Raelynn froze. A voice repeated her name in a whisper...

Her heart pounded out a staccato rhythm against her rib cage. Had her stalker found her?

Raelynn dropped down, crouching low. Scanning the ground, she searched for anything she could use as a weapon. Her fingers curled around a stick with a reasonable point on the end.

A noise startled her. Before she could look, a hand came over her mouth. A voice in her ear said, "Don't panic. I'm here to help, but if you scream, the shooter will have no problem killing us both." The deep baritone traveled over Raelynn and through her, even though she'd never met the man before. "Understand?"

She nodded, realizing she had no options. She had to hope this man could be trusted because she was handing over her life...

All my love to Brandon, Jacob and Tori, who are the great loves of my life. To Samantha for the bright shining light that you are.

To Babe, my hero, for being my best friend, greatest love and my place to call home. I love you with everything that I am. Always and forever.

Last but not least, to Alvaro Montelongo for your incredible kindness and for making us feel so welcome in San Francisco. And to JP Simoens for sharing your space and your art with us—you are so incredibly talented!

TRAPPED IN TEXAS

USA TODAY Bestselling Author

BARB HAN

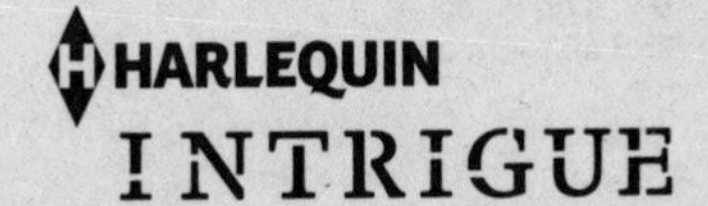

PLEASE RECYCLE · THIS PRODUCT IS RECYCLABLE

Recycling programs for this product may not exist in your area.

ISBN-13: 978-1-335-58265-2

Trapped in Texas

For questions and comments about the quality of this book, please contact us at CustomerService@Harlequin.com.

Harlequin Enterprises ULC
22 Adelaide St. West, 41st Floor
Toronto, Ontario M5H 4E3, Canada
www.Harlequin.com

Printed in U.S.A.

USA TODAY bestselling author **Barb Han** lives in north Texas with her very own hero-worthy husband, three beautiful children, a spunky golden retriever/standard poodle mix and too many books in her to-read pile. In her downtime, she plays video games and spends much of her time on or around a basketball court. She loves interacting with readers and is grateful for their support. You can reach her at barbhan.com.

Books by Barb Han

Harlequin Intrigue

The Cowboys of Cider Creek

Rescued by the Rancher
Riding Shotgun
Trapped in Texas

A Ree and Quint Novel

Undercover Couple
Newlywed Assignment
Eyewitness Man and Wife
Mission Honeymoon

An O'Connor Family Mystery

Texas Kidnapping
Texas Target
Texas Law
Texas Baby Conspiracy
Texas Stalker
Texas Abduction

Visit the Author Profile page at Harlequin.com.

CAST OF CHARACTERS

Raelynn Simmons—Is she being targeted by a stalker or a murderer?

Sean Hayes—Taking one last assignment might prove deadly for this former army ranger.

Anton Miles—Is this tech worker a stalker?

Mitch Razor—The founder and owner of Razor-Sharp Worldwide Security might secretly be Raelynn's father.

Drake Johnson—How far will this rival go to get back at Mitch for past mistakes?

Erik and Ashley Bradshaw—This couple's financial interest in Raelynn might not be all that is at stake.

Rudy Cannon—How far will this stage manager go to cover a gambling problem?

Chapter One

Sean Hayes moved with ease on the trail leading to Hamilton Pool in Austin, Texas, despite the nerve damage in his hands causing them to twitch. It was early December and surprisingly warm outside. A weather front was due in a couple of days that was about to turn the temperatures upside down and was expected to last through the weekend. Sean hated the cold about as much as having a last-minute assignment dumped in his lap. He'd been close to the location of the spotting, so he'd agreed to make a detour instead of hitting the highway. Considering he was about to take indefinite leave from the private security firm where he worked, he figured he owed them one more. Mitch Razor and the team had been nothing but good to him.

"Tell me again who I'm looking for and how she is connected to the agency," he said discreetly into the microphone attached to the button on his jacket sleeve.

"Best as I can tell she's somehow related to Mitch," Josiah Grady said. Sean and Josiah worked well together. He would miss his work buddy. The thought struck him as strange considering the two had worked together three years now and had never so much as gone out for a beer. *Acquaintance* might be a better word when he really thought about it. In this line of work, making friends wasn't exactly a priority but he had no doubt each member of the organization would have his back. Most of the employees of Razor-Sharp Worldwide Security came from jobs they no longer wanted to talk about, or maybe they never did in the first place. The company hired more than its fair share of ex-military and the assignments kept them on the road and mostly alone.

"I take it we don't know how," he said quietly. The nondisclosure agreement alone meant Sean could never openly speak about what he really did. But this assignment just took on a whole new level of importance.

"Mitch isn't saying," Josiah stated as Sean hiked along the pathway, passing families with young children and both leashed and unleashed dogs. A redhead caught his eye. Was she the one? He double-checked his cell phone. The woman in the picture was wearing a baseball cap, but even with most of her fiery locks tucked inside, she was unmistakable. The body type was a perfect match, roughly five feet seven inches that was mostly made up of long and lean legs. A heart-shaped face and big hazel eyes were more proof he'd found who he came looking for. He discreetly snapped a pic so facial recognition software could confirm the match.

The response took less than five seconds. *Target verified.*

Sean had been given this one last assignment before heading home to the successful family cattle ranch after his brothers Callum and Rory had made the call that it would be best if everyone showed. Callum, the oldest of six, had been the first to send word after checking out the situation for himself. Their mother Marla had asked her children to come back to Cider Creek in order to take their rightful places. No one had jumped at the chance. Their overbearing grandfather was to blame. All of the disagreements and hostility should be water under the bridge now that Duncan Hayes was gone, and yet facing the ranch again was proving more difficult than it probably should.

Sean's job was classified, or the next best thing to it, and a much better fit than cattle ranching under Duncan had been. Private security was a lucrative business. Mitch Razor was one of the best. If someone needed to disappear without a trace, they called Mitch. If someone needed protection, they called Mitch. If someone needed to find someone, they called Mitch. Sean located folks. He would help people disappear. But he refused to work protection details. Not after Kandahar.

"It's her," he said, low and under his breath. "Out here, there isn't a whole lot I can do without drawing attention." Attention wasn't ideal. Otherwise, he could throw her over his shoulder caveman-style to get her back to his SUV—although, the determined set to her chin told him she was a fighter.

"Roger that," Josiah agreed.

This was a game of patience. Sean needed to stay just enough out of sight not to cause her to notice him but close enough to keep an eye on which way she turned. He stopped long enough to take a knee and fake tying his hiking boot. He kept a rucksack in the backseat of his SUV, which he'd tossed on his back to further the illusion he was on a trail hike. Having the boots on hand had been a lucky bonus find.

"You coming back after leave?" Josiah asked. The question caught Sean off guard as a guy came running past. The dude almost trampled Sean. There was something about the runner that fired off warning flares inside Sean's brain.

On closer examination, he noticed a couple of things. One, the guy wasn't wearing a backpack. Two, he had on a whole lot of black—jeans, shirt, shoes. Three, he wore running shoes instead of boots. Plus, sunglasses. They wouldn't be a huge surprise except for the fact he was trying to sell himself as a jogger.

There was, however, something that caused Sean's blood to run cold. His eyes were locked on to Sean's target.

"I have competition," Sean said into his microphone as he scanned the area, ignoring Josiah's question. As it was, he could cut into the trees and run full force around the back to get to the redhead first. The other option was to shoot his competition. "Give me her name."

"Roger that. The target's first name is Raelynn," Josiah stated.

In a split second, Sean calculated the odds of getting to Raelynn first. He would fail. He could, however, slow down the runner long enough to convince Raelynn her safety depended on listening to everything he said to do.

Sean reached inside his rucksack for his stun gun as he took off running. He could comfortably hit a mark at twenty feet out in these conditions without risking hitting an innocent bystander. A clearing up ahead might provide the perfect opportunity to get off a clean shot.

The runner glanced backward in time to catch Sean staring right at him. This scene was about to get ugly.

"Get down and stay down," he urged a family of four as he bolted right past them. The youngest son who looked to be about four years old clasped his hands together, index fingers pointing outward like a gun. The visual was all Runner needed to start zigzagging through trees. The move made getting off a clean shot next to impossible and Sean only had himself to thank. He bit back a string of curses.

Raelynn caught on to the commotion, too. Like a startled deer, she broke into a dead run in the opposite direction. So, yeah, this day was going to hell in a handbasket faster than Sean could utter the words *bad idea.*

Since Runner was his first priority right now, Sean had to risk losing visual with his target. Branches slapped him in the face as he bolted through the trees, trying to get close enough to Runner to fire off a shot. The guy was quick on his feet but the stun gun would change that.

Other than general body type and description, Sean couldn't get close enough to see details like Runner's hair color or facial features. Not everything was lost, though. Sean was gaining on the guy.

Runner swiveled behind a tree. The turnaround happened so fast that it scarcely registered. The crack of a bullet split the air. Panicked screams echoed through the trees as Sean grabbed a tree trunk to put some mass in between him and shrapnel. Through sheer luck, Sean escaped picking metal fragments out of his body by inches. The voice in his earpiece was going nuts at this point. Josiah heard everything via the microphone pinned to Sean's shirt. Sean's panting, as well as the thunder of his hiking boots on hard terrain, must have been battering Josiah's ears. Plus, the shot fired. Anyone who'd worked in the military or law enforcement had the sound etched into their brains.

The worst part? Runner had disappeared.

GASPING FOR AIR, Raelynn Simmons pushed her legs long past the point her thighs burned. The sound of a gunshot echoed but she couldn't risk stopping to see what might be behind her. A few seconds could give her chaser time to catch up.

He'd found her. Whoever *he* was. She'd been on the down low ever since the close call in Fort Worth after her last show before pulling out of the tour. Opening for Texas Country had been the boost her career had desperately needed, and she was finally on the cusp of reaching so many people with her music. The thought of losing it all now over an obsessed stalker was a rock in her chest. Staying alive meant being on the run like a common criminal. There weren't a whole lot of other options. The cops couldn't keep her safe while on tour and she couldn't afford a personal bodyguard. The stalker had gotten past Texas Country's security team to steal her underwear and bra from her dressing room. The last FBI agent who spoke to her was a profiler. He'd informed her that the person stalking her wanted to possess her. The thought sent an icy chill racing down her spine. *Creep.*

Right now, she had a more immediate problem. How did she get out of her current situation alive?

The agent had assured her the stalker wouldn't try to kill her. He wanted her alive. A shiver rocked her body at the thought. Then came the last not-so-cryptic message that had been sent to her fan club manager. *Get back on stage or die.* According to the agent, the stalker's fixation had to do with a fantasy about her while she was performing. If he couldn't have that, she was no use to him any longer. Rather than move on, someone who was fixated would see her as the problem.

Her problems didn't end there. Backing out of the tour had caused her to rack up enemies in the business. Even when the dust settled and this creep was locked behind bars—which she could only pray would be soon—all the momentum she'd gained in her career would have slipped away each week she couldn't be on tour. Every canceled show set her back months—if not years—of hard-earned career growth. Her reputation was tanking by the minute, and she couldn't do anything about it without putting her life at risk.

Since the law couldn't do anything to prevent a crime, they'd been of very little help to her. Checking on her past complaints netted the same result: a detective promised to call if there was a development. There was a serious flaw in his logic. If the guy struck again, she would be the first to know.

Raelynn kept running even as her lungs clawed for air. Pandemonium had followed the gunshot; people had scattered like buckshot and there were enough folks around that she had a real chance of getting out of this situation alive. At least, she hoped.

Risking a glance, a small moment of relief struck as she saw that she was alone. For how long, she had no idea. She'd lost her bearings and had no idea where she was in the park. Could she circle back?

The thought of running into the shooter, or the man who'd popped up to chase him before he could have possibly known about the threat, sent another icy chill racing down her back. There'd been too many close calls before she'd gone into hiding and too many since then for her to let her guard down. It was only a matter of time before the odds worked against her no matter how sharp, focused and vigilant she stayed. At some point, the probability he would find her would tip in his favor.

Then what?

Raelynn had no idea what this man ultimately wanted from her. The thought of a stalker sickened her to no end. Hiding at the preserve had been the only move, no matter how much she wanted to stand up and fight. This wasn't a run-of-the-mill playground bully she was facing. This guy meant business and he seemed locked onto one thing…her.

Cutting left, she ran deeper into the thicket. She'd been running for what seemed like forever now but was probably just a few minutes. The dry uplands were ahead, which meant the canyon would be eighty feet below. Being on higher ground would give her better visibility of the area. Another thought struck—a dark thought: it would also make her an easier target in some ways. She reminded herself not to get too lax as she rushed through the trees and branches slapped her face.

Blasting ahead, she ran smack into a spiderweb the size of Texas. Spitting and frantically wiping her face to remove the last remnants of the cobweb while doing a dance no one needed to see, she froze when she heard a male voice coming from deeper in the woods. Her heart pounded out a staccato rhythm against the inside of her rib cage as she heard him repeat her name in a whisper.

She'd made too much noise thanks to the unexpected run-in with nature. Had he found her?

Raelynn dropped down, crouching low enough to

make herself a small target. Scanning the ground, she searched for anything she could use either to stay hidden or to fight back. Feeling around, her fingers located a stick with a reasonable point on the end. She grabbed it and a blunt rock that fit comfortably inside her palm.

The footsteps grew louder as she focused on making her palms warm—a trick she'd learned in yoga class a few years back to help calm her. She'd taken the class to learn how to counter the anxious feelings that always seemed to creep up on her when she tried to get close to anyone. Her relationship track record could best be described as a battlefield littered with carcasses—tough imagery when she really thought about it, but an honest assessment, as much as she hated to admit it.

Raelynn listened as her gaze skimmed the thicket. The voice sounded hushed.

Reality dawned that her stalker wouldn't exactly want to draw attention to himself by talking. Plus, who would he be talking to anyway? As far as she could tell, he'd been alone.

A father shielding a small child emerged, cautiously scanning the area. His gaze landed on her and he immediately put his arm in front of his kid. Raelynn didn't spend a whole lot of time around humans tinier than four feet tall, but this one looked to be around kindergarten age. The maternal gene seemed to have skipped her. The only tangible thing she ever connected with was music.

The fact Pappa Bear over there had spotted her

meant she was easy to see. Before anyone else came out of those trees, she needed to move.

The sun was bearing down on that spot on the crown of her head that always seemed to draw the heat. She moved deeper into the trees for relief since the temperature was climbing during this unseasonable heat wave.

A noise to her left startled her. Before she could look over, someone lunged at her. A hand covered her mouth before she could scream. And a voice in her ear said, "Don't panic. I'm here to help but if you scream the shooter will have no problem killing us both. Understand?"

She nodded while evaluating her options.

"If I move my hand, do you promise not to make a peep?" the strong male voice asked. His deep baritone traveled over her and through her, despite never having met him before.

She nodded, realizing she had no options. At this point, she had to hope he could be trusted, because right now, her life was in his hands.

Chapter Two

Sean looked deep into Raelynn's eyes, unsure of what he was searching for exactly other than some indication he could remove his hand from her mouth. He'd abandoned his search for Runner, doubling back instead to locate her.

"Are we good?" he asked one more time for reassurance.

She nodded agreement, so he took the risk and removed his hand, dropping it to his side while holding her gaze. A jolt of electricity rocketed through him as he locked on to those hazel eyes of hers. Chalking it up to the dangers around them and not a real attraction happening between them, he said, "I'm here to help get you out of this alive."

She clamped her mouth shut, giving a slight nod instead of speaking.

Sean couldn't help noticing the fact her face features favored Mitch, but that could just be his imagination running away with him. Into the small microphone, he said, "I have the asset and we're heading out."

Confused didn't begin to cover the look on Raelynn's face. He didn't blame her and didn't have time to explain. Later, she would get the full rundown. They weren't out of the woods in any sense of the expression.

"Roger that," Josiah confirmed. His all-business tone was tinged with relief.

"No time to talk," he said to her.

"Let's get out of here. Preferably alive," she said in a surprise move.

Clasping their hands together, he moved methodically through the trees. As they advanced deeper into the thicket, he listened for any signs of being followed. The gunshot had sent everyone running. Law enforcement would flood the place soon, if park police weren't already on the scene. Sean needed to get Raelynn away from this area before either of them could be identified by witnesses.

At this point, local cops were of no use to Sean or the mission. A stealth extraction was the best play. Witnesses would be able to give local law enforcement the rundown of what had just happened. No doubt someone had the scene on their camera phone. The incident would most likely be on the news in a matter of minutes, which would make it that much more difficult to get away.

Although Sean's actions would pin him as someone who was trying to stop the shooter, he didn't need the visibility in his line of work. Flying under the radar had kept him alive for many years and with a degree of sanity intact.

At least he knew the way to his SUV, making his own trail back. The shooter should be long gone by now. Sean wouldn't take any chances. He had yet to lose an asset and had no intentions of starting now.

Weaving his way back to his vehicle, he figured Raelynn was in shock. Civilians didn't usually handle this type of situation well. They weren't used to bullets flying past their heads or bad men popping out of nowhere.

Hold on a second. Sean realized why Raelynn looked so familiar. She was the up-and-coming country singer who'd gone missing from her tour a while ago—maybe even five or six months, if memory served. There'd been some news of a stalker as he recalled. But why had Mitch assigned the case when she didn't appear to want to be found?

Was Raelynn Simmons Mitch's daughter? She looked too close to Mitch's age, but he'd learned a long time ago looks could be deceiving. Sibling?

Considering Sean had been working for his boss for the past five years, he should know more about the man's family history. At this point, he had no idea where Mitch lived or if he even had a family. To be fair, he didn't know a whole lot about anyone's personal life at Razor-Sharp. Everyone seemed to prefer keeping work separate from their homelife. Sean figured most of the men and women where he worked were single and wanted to keep it that way, much like himself. Some people were born to be alone.

Methodically, he moved around the perimeter of the park. It was nightfall by the time they reached his

SUV. Josiah had gone dark, which didn't mean his coworker wasn't listening and at the ready if needed. The lot was mostly vacant.

Sean moved to the passenger side of his vehicle and opened the door for Raelynn. His suspicion she was somehow related to Mitch grew by the minute. First of all, there was a resemblance. It wasn't a mirror image, but it was close enough. Second, why else would they be extracting her from the park? What could Mitch possibly have to gain by protecting her if she was a random person?

It wasn't his job to ask or answer questions, even though he saw plenty brewing behind the most incredible pair of hazel eyes. He circled around the front of the SUV, scanning the area just to ensure there would be no more surprises. A thought haunted him: Raelynn had been fine on her own before he'd shown up at the park. Had he led Runner right to her?

The unpleasant thought was sobering as he claimed the driver's seat. Guilt stabbed him in the center of his chest like a knife. The air suddenly seemed like it had been sucked out of the vehicle. Breathing was hard. Sean pushed the button to turn on the ignition while forcing a smile.

"What's going on? Who are you? And what just happened?" Raelynn asked. She was putting up a brave front despite the shock that had been written all over her face and was present in her tone.

"You have a right to answers to all of those questions," he reassured her as he put the gearshift in reverse. "I'm certainly not here to hurt you, as I assume you already figured out."

"I wouldn't be sitting here otherwise," she quipped before crossing her arms over her chest. It was a defensive move that indicated she was feeling vulnerable. Understandable given the circumstances.

"Right," he said as he navigated onto the road and headed east. "I'm not at liberty to answer any of those questions no matter how much I realize this statement seems unfair to you. You're not being held captive, so you're free to go at any time. Tell me to stop and I will. Although, I won't want to, and I'd have to fill out a full report as to how I let an asset go."

"Asset?" she parroted. "Why do you sound like some kind of CIA operative?"

"I can assure you that I'm not," he said. "I'm Sean, by the way."

"Is that your real name?" she asked.

He couldn't help but smile a little at the question.

"That's affirmative," he said.

"Correction to my earlier statement," she said. "You sound like you're ex-military."

"Right again," he confirmed. It was the least he could do considering he'd just plucked her out of the woods and hurried her into his vehicle. "Army Ranger."

"Are you allowed to tell me that?" she asked with a little more ire in her voice than he expected.

The corners of his lips upturned once again.

"Probably not," he confirmed. "As long as you don't give me up, we're cool."

"Do you happen to know who that man was back there?" she asked, pinching the bridge of her nose like she was trying to stem one helluva headache.

"That, I can't tell you," he said.

"Can't or won't?" she persisted, and he realized she was not only sharp but observant—a lethal combination to someone in his line of work. *Former* line of work, he corrected.

"Does it matter?" he asked, figuring that her knowing the answer wouldn't change the fact she wasn't going to get the information she wanted.

"It does to me," she said with an honesty that cracked a bit of the casing around his heart.

"Can't," he said as she nodded.

"Figures," she said. "I'm finally rescued by a knight in shining armor and all he can tell me is his first name." Her sense of humor reminded him a whole lot of Mitch's.

"Can I ask a question?" Sean turned the tables since she'd assessed the situation accurately.

"*You* want to ask *me* something?" she asked, clearly caught off guard with the change in direction. There was an indignation to her voice that probably shouldn't make him respect her even more. So far, she was proving brave in a situation that would decimate others.

"Yes," he confirmed, figuring he might as well go for broke. He would turn her in at the office and then head home to the ranch, never to see her again.

He might as well ask his question now while they were forced to be together for a little while longer during the ride back to headquarters.

"Shoot," she said, before seeming to catch her word choice and possibly wanting to reel it back in. "What I mean is…what do you want to know?"

"Who your parents are," he said. "Which might sound strange but—"

"I'd tell you if I knew," she said, interrupting him with a harsh sigh. "I'm an orphan."

Those three words, along with the tinge of sadness in her voice, struck as hard as a physical blow.

"WHERE ARE WE GOING?" Raelynn asked when Sean didn't respond to her last comment. Being an orphan was all she'd ever known, and she rarely ever spoke about the past. Why she'd confided in this stranger was beyond her. Then again, she'd just had a close call and there was something about facing death that made her want to have a connection with someone. The past few months had proven to be the loneliest of her life and it was nice someone had her back for a change.

"Back to the home office," he answered. His voice was a low rumble in his chest. There was something about his tone that made her think he was conflicted. Was he supposed to be quiet and deliver her to her destination?

"Where is that?" she asked.

"Outside of San Antonio," he stated, answering in as few words as possible.

"No offense, but I think I deserve to know what's going on, where you're taking me and on whose command," she said, appealing to his logical nature. He seemed like the kind of person who would appreciate a straightforward approach.

"I would tell you if I knew why I was sent to pick you up," he said, and there was another emotion present in his voice when he spoke this time. The man was all dark, danger, and…excitement? Maybe *excitement* wasn't the right word, but being in the SUV with him caused a dozen butterflies to release in her stomach. She would chalk it up to escaping death but there was more to it—*attraction* was a strong word, and yet it seemed to fit the circumstances well.

Sean had to be six feet three or four inches tall. The man had a body that would fit nicely on a billboard in Times Square as an underwear model. He had stacked muscles on top of lean hips. There was something improbable and unattainable about him. He carried himself with confidence that bordered on arrogance and told her that he knew how to handle himself in any situation. His black-as-pitch hair was cut military short. His hawk-like nose only added to his looks—looks that wouldn't be considered pretty despite thick lips and a chiseled jawline. This man was devastatingly handsome, despite the fact his white teeth weren't perfectly straight and he had a two-inch scar above his left eye. Speaking of eyes, his were a sun-kissed honey brown and softened the otherwise dark features on his intense face.

"Is that how it works?" she asked. "Because you

don't seem like the type of person who blindly follows orders."

His face broke into a wide smile at the non-compliment, which only served to make him more interesting.

"The key word there is *blind*," he said after a couple of seconds passed.

"That's fair," she admitted, wondering if she could get any information out of him. His demeanor said that he was also the type of person who could be tortured to within an inch of his life and still not give up so much as his last name. Speaking of which... "Considering you just saved my life, are you authorized to tell me your last name?"

"Hayes," he said, widening the smile.

"Of *the* Hayes family?" she asked, not bothering to hide her shock. Why on earth would one of the most successful cattle ranchers work for what could only be a shadow organization when he came from the kind of money that could buy a small country?

Now he laughed, which made her a little indignant.

"I'm just saying that you could do anything you wanted with your...background," she said for lack of a better word. "Why do this job?"

"Seemed like a good idea at the time and I wasn't ready to go back to Cider Creek where I'm from," he said with a shrug. It was then she noticed a slight tremor in his right hand. He pulled it off the steering wheel before flexing and releasing it a couple of times. When the tremor seemed to stop, he returned his hand to the wheel. His grip caused his knuckles to turn white, and all amusement dropped from his features.

Summing him up, he was clearly ex-military. And exceptional at keeping secrets.

A man with the background of Sean Hayes wouldn't want to display weakness. Raelynn took note that he clenched his back teeth like he was trying to get his body back under control. Her heart went out to him for what he must have experienced to cause damage to his hands. The scar above his eye said he'd been face-to-face with death, probably on more than one occasion. Was that the reason he seemed to be comfortable with what had just happened while she felt like a total wreck inside?

"How long have you worked at your job?" she asked, before adding, "Talking helps calm my nerves." Then, she felt the need to explain. "I'm a musician and songwriter, so I'm not used to these scrapes with death or having men swoop out of seemingly nowhere to save the day. My world is a whole lot calmer than that. Or, at least, it was until recently and now I'm just trying to stay alive long enough for the law to figure out who is stalking me and lock him behind bars."

"Singer," he corrected and there was an emotion in his voice that she couldn't quite pinpoint. Sadness? Regret? Neither made sense considering he'd done his job. She was in his vehicle. They were on the way to what she assumed was his headquarters, whatever that meant. And he was in the process of accomplishing his mission.

"That's right," she said, more than a little impressed that a person like him would know who she was. Being recognized was still a little foreign to her, especially outside the music world where she was most well-known. Random people on the street had just started coming up to her with surprised looks on their faces, still timid about asking if she was Raelynn Simmons.

The fame side of her work took some getting used to considering she mainly wanted to write songs. Singing took second place.

"I'm still a little confused why anyone would come to your organization and hire you to save me," she said. "How long have you been following me? Days? Weeks?"

Sean took in a breath like he was considering his options.

"I literally just got a call a few hours ago asking if I'd take on this mission since I was close by and you'd been spotted," he said. "My job was to pick you up and convince you to come into the office. However, the shooter changed my mind."

"Oh," she said as she stared at him, realizing there was something else on his mind.

"There's a high probability that I'm the reason the guy found you in the first place," he said with frustration and disgust. "So, I'm sticking around until I find out who the hell hired us because right now my guess is that my agency has been duped. Since

I got the assignment and this is now on my head, I need to find out what is really going on or I won't sleep at night."

Raelynn was speechless for a long moment as she tried to process the update. There was almost too much to unpack there as she dug through the layers of his admission.

"Are we getting close?" she asked as he turned off the highway and on to a small road.

He nodded.

Now that her world had been turned upside down again, she hoped they could find answers at Sean's office. She had plenty of questions for the person in charge.

Chapter Three

Security was tight everywhere at the office compound, none of which was visible unless someone knew where to look and what they were looking for. The minute Sean's front tires hit the gravel road a sensor was tripped. The alarm automatically turned cameras on. Facial recognition software matched the driver or passenger to employee files, in which case the alarm system stopped, thereafter verifying body temperature to ensure the employee was alive.

The other layers required human intervention and meant there'd been a breach. Since Sean was technically still an employee, they should be fine.

"Mitch is the name of my boss," Sean said as he parked in front of the two-story brick building, also known as headquarters. He didn't think about how strange it might seem to an outsider that he knew so little about the man he worked for, not to mention his coworkers. This line of work wasn't like having a corporate gig where folks went out to happy hour three nights a week with people from the office.

"Does he have a last name?" she asked. It was

dark by now but there was light enough in the SUV for him to see her clearly.

"Razor," he supplied, figuring it couldn't hurt. She would know soon enough anyway after they exited the vehicle and went inside. But first, he needed to get something off his chest. "I owe you an apology."

Her mouth opened and then clamped shut real fast. Her lips compressed into a thin line as though she was doing her best not to speak her mind. It would be better if she went ahead and blasted him for the mistake.

"You couldn't have known," she said after a few beats of silence.

"It's my job to know," he corrected. "And I'm usually the best. No one should be able to slip past my radar or use me to get to an asset."

"This whole finding me bit might have been a setup like you said," she pointed out. "That isn't technically your responsibility. I'm guessing Mitch should have vetted any persons interested in finding me."

"True," he said, and yet it was impossible not to blame himself for what had happened. Because of him, she could have been killed. A flashback to the innocent villagers who'd died under his watch caused a sharp pain in between his temples. He tried to mentally shake it off as he refocused. "The bottom line is that I failed you and put you at risk when I was supposed to extract and protect. It doesn't matter where the link broke in the chain."

"It does to me," she said softly. There was a forgiving note in her tone that he didn't deserve.

"Well, it shouldn't," he said before reaching for the handle as he threw his shoulder into the door. Sean exited the SUV and then came around the front of the vehicle to open the passenger side. He knew she was fully capable of opening her own door. However, he was brought up to offer, and the fact she waited for him signaled a green light for the chivalry that had been ingrained in him.

She thanked him and then folded her arms across her chest, a sure sign she was feeling vulnerable again. Part of him wanted to warn her that she might be about to meet her father for the first time, but he had no idea if the information would be welcomed or accurate. It wasn't his place to interfere with a family if that was the case. Plus, it was just a hunch at this point. She was connected to the boss in some way. Josiah had said it flat-out before being sent off on another mission overseas to locate a missing child. Whether or not Mitch was her father was still unanswered.

The thought of walking away from a job that had probably saved his life after his military service was another physical blow. This was the last time he would be driving onto the compound or walking through these doors—or drinking the strong dark roast that wasn't bad if the pot was fresh but everyone still drank when it tasted like scorched mud.

It shouldn't strike him as a missed opportunity that he didn't know his coworkers beyond these walls. All that had mattered was whether or not he could count on them during a mission. Every last person employed by Mitch was top-notch. There'd been no birthday celebrations or cake parties in the small kitchenette. There'd been no hanging out after hours. And there'd been no company outings to baseball games or Putt-Putt. And yet, this still felt like walking away from family. Shouldn't he feel that way about the ranch?

After closing the door to the SUV, Raelynn surprised him by leaning against the vehicle instead of moving forward.

"What am I about to walk into?" she asked. Several vehicles were parked in the lot. She motioned toward them. "I'm at a loss here. I've had a stalker essentially run me off my own tour and now you show up based on someone's command." She threw her hands up in the air. The frustrated look in her eyes was about all he could see in the darkness. It was past dinner and his stomach reminded him that food was a good idea soon. She must be starving, too. The look in her eyes also reminded him that she was all alone in this. He couldn't imagine being on the other side of a conversation like this one and she'd shown enormous trust in him by getting into his vehicle—hell, allowing him to lead her out of the thicket had been brave on her part, too.

"We can go inside or get back in my vehicle and take off right now," he said by way of concession. "However, if you want to know what's going on we have to walk through those doors, where my boss is waiting." He studied her to see if he was making inroads. She scraped her teeth across her bottom lip, and he could tell that she was considering his words. "You say the word and we're gone at any moment."

She shifted her weight from one foot to the other. More signs he was making progress. His cell phone buzzed, startling her. He half expected her to bolt.

"What will you do once we're inside?" she asked, blinking up at him with eyes that studied him like he was a final exam and she was about to fail the course.

"I'll stay," he said. "I already told you that I brought danger to you. There's no way in hell I plan to allow that to happen again. I'm here until you tell me to leave, or until this thing is over."

It was a promise he shouldn't make because he had to break another one to follow through with it. His family would understand if he was a couple of days late. He could explain that something came up for work. *Work.* He bit back the irony they had no idea what he did for a living.

"What if your boss tells you to go?" she asked.

"I'll defer to you instead," he promised.

"Okay," she said. "I'll go inside and hear your boss out. But that doesn't mean I'll go along with anything or stay longer than ten minutes."

"Sounds good to me," he said before adding, "I won't put you in harm's way again. Not if I can help it."

"Good," she countered. "Because you're the only friend I've got right now."

"Razor-Sharp is the name of the organization," he said.

She nodded with a look of appreciation in her eyes that he'd trusted her with the information.

It was probably finding a kindred spirit that cracked more of the hard casing around his heart. Two broken souls crossing paths, or some poetic nonsense like that. But there was no way he was walking away from Raelynn until he knew she was safe. Like it or not, she'd just found her new best friend.

"Let's go inside and hear Mitch out," he said to a tentative nod. "It'll be okay. I'm not going anywhere."

Standing here in the dark, breathing in her flowers-after-a-spring-rain scent reminded him how much he missed being out on the land and how lonely he'd been in recent years.

"Promise?" she asked, looking deep into his eyes like she could see right through him.

"Yes."

THERE WAS STILL something about the dark that made an almost-thirty-year-old Raelynn cringe. She'd managed to block out the nightmares years ago, but the last time she'd startled awake from a thunderstorm had taken her right back to those awful years spent at the orphanage. Channeling all those emotions into her songwriting had kept her sane all these years. Having to step out of her rising country music career to go into hiding infuriated her. Since she realized she couldn't have a career if she was dead, she'd reluctantly disappeared.

Considering Sean was the only person she knew here—and she used the term *knew* loosely—it probably shouldn't have surprised her that she instinctively reached for his hand. He didn't strike her as someone who took giving his word lightly.

"Then I'm ready," she said to him, still processing his admission of bringing her stalker right to her. There was no way he would have done that on purpose. Instinct, or the foreign-feeling connection to him that defied explanation, confirmed he'd had the best of intentions. This seemed like a good time to remind herself the two of them weren't friends, no matter how much her heart argued. Sean Hayes was doing his job, a job he seemed very good at. She hoped so, she thought with a sharp sigh, because her life depended on it.

As soon as he opened the door, he dropped her hand. It occurred to her that he would want to keep up a professional front to his boss. She felt the air cool around them as she followed him inside. The brick two-story had an open-concept design, with desks lining the walls of what would be the living area and a long glass conference table that could seat eight directly in the middle of the room.

The second they entered the room, a man stood up and turned around to face them. "'Bout time you came inside, Hayes. I was beginning to wonder what was going on out there." He winked.

Sean laughed, but the moment of levity didn't

reach his eyes. He introduced her to Mitch, who was tall and muscled. Muscles, it seemed, were a job requirement at Razor-Sharp.

"I'm a fan of your music," Mitch said before walking over and extending a hand. An emotion passed behind his eyes that she couldn't quite pinpoint. The look on his face sent up a few warning flares.

After the handshake, she instinctively moved partially behind Sean. He seemed to pick up on her trepidation.

"Maybe we should sit down at the conference table and talk," Sean said, motioning toward the glass top.

"Good idea," Mitch said. She studied him. The red tint to his otherwise brown hair registered somewhere in the back of her mind as interesting. He was tall—not Sean tall, but tall. Mitch looked at her like he knew her, but she was drawing a blank.

"Have we met before?" she asked him as he walked toward the table, figuring it was always easier to address the elephant in the room rather than ignore it.

"It's possible," he said, with a hopeful quality to his voice that also caught her off guard.

Sean reached back for her hand, and then squeezed as though offering reassurance. He stopped at the back of the black-and-chrome chair, and then turned toward her. His full attention was like standing with the sun to her face on a warm spring day.

"Are you hungry?" he asked.

"Starved," she admitted, surprising herself with her honesty.

"I bet we can dig up something to heat in the kitchen," he said.

"Help yourself," Mitch said a little too quickly, a little too eager. That was the thing she couldn't put her finger on earlier—he was too enthusiastic for the circumstances. He was masking it somewhat, and she figured he was usually a cool cucumber considering he ran a place like this.

She thanked him and followed Sean into the adjoining room. The kitchen was separated from the living room by an oblong granite island. There were a few chairs pushed up to the side closest to her.

"Do you want to take a seat while I look around?" he asked, motioning toward a barstool.

"Sure," she responded, as Mitch seemed to be gathering up files in the background. "But first, can I grab a cup of coffee?"

"Help yourself," Sean said as she came around the island.

There were mugs hanging off a decorative metal tree next to the pot. The coffee smelled fresh. She would count that as a win under the circumstances. She pulled two mugs after a quick glance toward Sean answered her question about whether or not he wanted a cup. Based on his quick nod and smile, he was all in.

"How do you take yours?" she asked after filling a pair of mugs.

"Black is good," he said as he rummaged through the fridge.

Palming her mug, she rolled it around between her palms, hoping the warmth could somehow reach deep inside her now that the AC hit her full force. Surprisingly, she felt safe for the first time in months. It had everything to do with Sean.

"How about I heat frozen pizza?" Sean asked.

"Sounds good to me," she said, taking a seat across the granite as Mitch joined Sean in the kitchen.

"I should have asked if you wanted a cup of coffee as I'm topping mine off," he said. She glanced at his left hand and didn't see a gold band. Neither man seemed to be married—or they didn't like to show it considering their line of work.

"I have questions," she said to Mitch while Sean busied himself preheating the oven and opening a couple of boxes. He located a couple of round pans next. He moved with athletic grace, despite the simple cooking task.

"It's understandable," he said. "So do I."

"What happened?" Sean asked, turning to his boss. "The mission went south and I'm asking myself how I could have let it."

"I'm checking into the background of the person who hired us," Mitch admitted. "Despite our normal protocols, this one slipped right through without raising any red flags. I'll debrief you both fully in a minute."

"We're here right now," Sean said. She could scarcely hold back a smile at his impatience. She felt the same.

"I see that," Mitch said with a surprising amount of patience. "But there's something more personal I'd like to discuss with Raelynn before we get started. Do you mind stepping out of the room for a few minutes?"

Sean finished unwrapping the pizzas, placed them on the round pans and then into the oven. He turned around and locked gazes with her. "Is that what you want?"

"No," she said emphatically before turning to Mitch. "Whatever you have to say to me can be said in front of Sean."

"You sure about that?" Mitch's eyebrow shot up.

"One-hundred-percent certain," she confirmed.

Mitch took in a sharp breath.

"I'm currently in the process of determining if you're my daughter," he said.

Those words nearly floored Raelynn. She practically had to pick her jaw up off the tile floor. "What?"

"Raelynn, I might be your father." Mitch shot an apologetic look as she tried to form words into questions.

"That's impossible," she said. "I'm an orphan. The nuns at the orphanage said my parents are dead. That was years ago."

"That might have been a lie," he said, with the kind of certainty in his voice that told her everything she thought she knew about her past was about to change forever.

Chapter Four

“How long have you known about me?”

Raelynn crossed her arms over her chest, signaling she felt vulnerable again. Sean bit back a curse, unsure as to why her comfort mattered to him so much.

“A couple of months now,” Mitch admitted.

“Are you serious?” she asked with a mix of frustration and disdain. “I’ve been stalked for a couple of months and then you come out of the woodwork?” She shook her head. “This can’t be real.”

“I owe you an apology,” Mitch began. “I’ll do whatever it takes to make this right.”

“Why are you interested in me now?” she asked, leaning her hip against the counter.

“You might be in danger because of me,” he stated. “I take that seriously.” Mitch had never come across as nervous in any situation or meeting in the years Sean had known his boss. Seeing the tension on his face as he tapped his heel on the floor was new territory. “And…”

Mitch took a deep breath.

"If I have a daughter out there somewhere, I'd like to know who she is and, possibly, have some kind of connection," he continued on a sharp sigh.

Raelynn seemed to take it all in for a few moments before responding. She'd just been handed a lot of information to process following a near-death experience and didn't look like she was in a hurry to speak.

"I appreciate what you're saying," she began, her stomach growling. "But my stalker doesn't fit the profile of someone wanting revenge on you."

"Do you mind filling me in on what's been happening?" he asked.

"I'm all for getting to the bottom of this situation as soon as possible, but we need to get food in our stomachs right now before Raelynn passes out," Sean interjected. Mitch was already nodding before Sean finished his sentence.

"I could eat," Raelynn said. "But I need to figure out my next move before it gets too late." He could imagine that she'd been flying under the radar by calculating her every move. She was good at being stealthy if it took Mitch a little time to find her. Sean didn't want to make the assumption *the apple didn't fall far from the tree* just yet. There'd been no DNA test to prove paternity. Based on Raelynn's age and Mitch's, he would have to have been very young when she was born, possibly not yet out of his teen years. It didn't rule out the possibility she was his daughter, but timing would be important.

"I'll just head over to my desk and see what I can

do to track down the person who hired us to find you," Mitch said.

"Which came first, by the way?" she asked. "Did someone hire you to track me down or were you already trying to find me?"

"I was hired," Mitch admitted. There was more to the story based on the look in his eyes, but he didn't seem ready to spit it out. For a second, Sean wondered if Raelynn was about to call Mitch on it. She didn't, so he assumed her hunger was getting the best of her.

"Interesting," Raelynn said quietly.

Mitch nodded. "I'll just make a few calls and get the ball rolling on a deeper investigation into who was really searching for you."

Sean realized the irony in having Raelynn's father find her for someone who wanted to do her harm, if that was truly the case. As far as revenge against Mitch might go, that would be poetic.

Knowing someone out there could be trying to get to Mitch through Raelynn sat hard in his gut. It meant real trackers were after her, people who wouldn't be as easy to shake as a typical obsessed stalker. Don't get him wrong—those weren't anything to take lightly either. The problem with professionals was that they had better skills and more experience, making them far more likely to achieve their goal.

The pizza didn't take long to make or eat. Sean opened a couple Cokes to go along with the meal rather than pour more coffee. It smelled burned, so he turned off the machine. She got up to clear her plate but he waved her off.

"I got this," he said, figuring she'd had enough excitement for one day.

"Is it weird that cleaning helps clear my head?" she asked as she stood up despite his protests. The kitchenette had a full-size dishwasher but she gathered the plates and then washed them by hand.

"It helps to do something normal again after a traumatic experience," he explained. "There's something about doing work with your hands that has the effect of emptying your brain."

"It's mindless, right?" she asked, but it was more statement than question. "And yet it seems to really be helping. Cleaning has always been my go-to when I've had a bad day. I'm not much of a cook, so I have to do something else with my hands."

"Working out usually does the trick for me," he said. "Doing anything physical helps."

"Makes sense," she said, then pointed to her forehead. "Hard to shut this off at times." She washed a plate and then rinsed it with warm water before stacking it on the counter. "I've been writing a lot of songs lately." She shook her head. "It's another way to get out all the frustration when I'm going through hard times, which I've had a lot of in my life."

He could only imagine what it must have been like growing up an orphan, considering he had five siblings. "Must have been tough growing up alone. It takes a special person to overcome a difficult past."

"The way I see it is that I didn't have another

choice but to figure it out," she said, moving on to drying the dishes before placing them one by one in the dishwasher. "No one can help what happens to them when they're little. But then, I don't know, you become a certain age and can no longer blame other people for the problems in your life. You have to step up at some point. Take responsibility for yourself."

"True," he agreed. "Too bad the rest of the world doesn't see it that way."

"There are exceptions, of course," she continued. "Some people can't help their situation and I don't blame them. I just believe it's up to us to make our lives better if we don't have someone else to do it for us." She tilted her head to one side, revealing her neckline. "You know?"

"I couldn't agree more," he said, which was exactly the reason he'd left the ranch for the military after high school. There was no reason to stick around a place where someone else thought they could tell Sean what to do and when to do it. His grandfather seemed committed to making Sean and his siblings' lives miserable, just like him. "I left home as soon as I could and joined the military in order to take control of my future."

"Aren't you a Hayes, though?" she asked on a shrug. "Wasn't your life handed to you on a silver platter?"

Sean had heard similar remarks for most of his young life. He was disappointed Raelynn fell into the same trap as others after believing she was special. An annoying voice in the back of his head pointed out that he was only hurt because he was starting to have feelings for her that he had no business feeling.

"Hey, sorry," she said as she dried the last glass. "I heard the way that sounded when it came out and it was a jerk move on my part. Every situation is different and just because people have money doesn't mean they have an easy life."

Her stock inched up after she backtracked and started making sense.

"People looking in from the outside usually believe the first thing you said," he explained. "Growing up with expectations from everyone, not to mention your grandfather after losing your father, isn't the barrel of laughs it's cracked up to be."

"I didn't mean to be offensive," she said, setting down the dish towel and then placing her hand on his forearm. "Really."

"Don't worry about it," he said, wondering how he'd suddenly become so sensitive. Was the thought of going back home opening old wounds? Wounds he wasn't ready to face?

This conversation was opening his eyes a little bit. He'd buried a few emotions down deep and then did his level best to forget all about them. Just thinking about losing his father put a lump in his throat. He'd been young when the car accident had taken his father's life. Duncan Hayes had said real men don't cry—they get back to work and keep their chin up. He'd been softer on Sean's sisters, but not by much. And not one of the Hayes children stuck around the ranch after graduating high school. Every last one of them had bolted the minute they could, and he didn't for the life of him know what any one of them was doing right now. He'd had messages from Callum, who was the oldest, messages Sean hadn't been quick to return. He'd skipped his grandfather's funeral last month, figuring he'd never been close enough with the man to care one way or the other.

And yet, a piece of him could admit that he wished their relationship had been better. Since beating himself up over walking away and never looking back wouldn't do any good, Sean shut it down. Regrets never changed anything. It was a virus that spread in the mind and body, consuming everything in its path.

"Everything okay?" Raelynn asked, standing two feet in front of him, snapping her fingers.

Sean blinked a couple of times and then gave himself a mental headshake.

"Yes," he responded, even though it wasn't.

RAELYNN WAS GOOD at reading people. Sean wasn't being truthful, but she didn't call him out on the fact, mainly because it was obvious to her that he didn't want to share what was going on. She got it. Sharing wasn't exactly her forte either. Just so he knew she understood him, she leaned in and said, "I'm here if you want to talk."

He opened his mouth to say something—something she imagined would be a protest—but he clamped it shut instead. A half smile curled the corners of his thick lips—lips she didn't need to focus on.

"I might just take you up on that someday," he said

barely above a whisper. The thought of her knowing him beyond the next couple of hours sent warmth rocketing through her. She figured he'd done his part and was most likely devising an exit plan at this point. The hope he might actually stick around took root and, surprisingly, made her feel safe. Raelynn had never needed anyone else. Recent events had her shaken but not broken. She still had faith in her skills to fly under the radar when needed, a skill she'd been honing her entire life. It was surprisingly easy to go unnoticed when she tucked her hair inside a ball cap, threw on a jacket and jeans and kept her head down. There was something she wished for, though, as thunder boomed and lightning cut across the night sky. Her guitar. "Is there any chance of being able to recover items from my campsite tomorrow?"

"Anything's possible," he said. "Is there something special that you had to leave behind?"

"My first guitar," she said. "I take it with me everywhere I go."

He nodded, and there was so much warmth in his otherwise unreadable eyes that her heart fisted in her chest. Her throat suddenly dried up and breathing was difficult.

"I scrimped and saved for that thing," she said on a shrug, trying to deflect some of the compassion coming at her. Getting attached to no one had been her go-to for survival since she was a kid, first in an orphanage and then in foster care. The minute she'd aged out of the system, she'd jumped right into a relationship with someone who wasn't good for her.

Tanner Voight was lead singer of The AXES. She'd been young and full of intense emotion during her years with Tanner. He'd been intent on keeping her under his thumb, though she hadn't seen it like that all those years ago. His possessiveness had been a sign of love to her.

How messed up was that?

With no positive role models to go by, she'd assumed it was normal for a boyfriend to check her phone every day to see if she was flirting with another guy. She'd assumed it was reasonable for someone to keep her tucked by his side at parties. And she'd assumed it was commonplace not to be able to leave the apartment unless her boyfriend knew where she was going and who she was going with. The fact those behaviors seemed ordinary to her at one point made her cringe now.

"I can't promise the weather won't do a number on it, but we'll get it back," Sean promised.

"The law might have found my campsite by now," she reasoned, after telling him the approximate location. "Would that make it evidence?"

"There was gun fire by a male shooter," he said after a thoughtful pause. She could almost see the wheels turning in his mind. "They won't be looking for a woman. They will examine your belongings if they find them, but there's no reason to consider anything evidence without a dead body on-site or reason to believe you were the shooter."

"That's a relief," she said on a sigh. "It probably sounds silly to someone like you, but the guitar means everything to me." It was the reason she carried it with her everywhere she went.

"Not really," he said as his deep timbre washed over her. The attraction caught her off guard because Sean Hayes wasn't her usual type. Not that he wasn't jaw-droppingly handsome and brooding, and had a body that even the fittest stars would kill for. Raelynn went for the brooding type. She'd always gone for other musicians and artists.

Had she always been drawn to guys she could keep at arm's length?

Looking back at her dating history, the answer was a hard yes. She'd spent time with guys who would end up on tour for a good chunk of the year. Many times, her tour was on the opposite schedule.

An irritating voice in the back of her mind pointed out those relationships were safe. No long-term commitment required. Was it true?

"Let me know when you're ready," Mitch said, walking over with a DNA test kit in his right hand.

"It's been a long day," she hedged. "Any chance we can do that in the morning after we discuss the stalker. My eyelids are closing on their own and I'm at the point of losing coherent sentences."

"Of course," Mitch said in a cheery tone. Too cheery. He was covering a little too enthusiastically. It dawned on Raelynn that he'd had time to think about what it might mean if their DNA matched up, whereas she'd just heard about the possibility. "Take your time." He paused before motioning toward a stairwell off the kitchen. "Sean can show you to a room upstairs."

"A hot shower and a soft bed sound amazing right now," she said, shutting down her curiosity about the man who could be her father. At present, she was in information overload despite the mounting questions about who and where her mother was. Could she sleep? Did it matter when she needed to be alone more than anything right now? Funny enough, *alone* had a new definition. It excluded all other people besides Sean Hayes. He brought comfort she didn't dare trust. Could he help find answers?

Chapter Five

Sean deposited Raelynn in one of four bedrooms upstairs before retreating downstairs. The sparkle in her eyes told him leaving as soon as possible was a good idea because the longer he stayed, the more difficult walking out the door would become. Plus, he had a mission.

"Where are you headed?" Mitch asked as Sean cut across the kitchen and toward the exit.

"I'll be back in a couple of hours," Sean said by way of explanation. He wasn't ready to detail his plans or discuss why retrieving Raelynn's guitar before the elements destroyed it had become his top priority.

"So, you're sticking around?" Mitch asked but it was more statement than question.

"I thought I might," Sean responded, stopping at the door. Mitch had given Sean work when his head was completely messed up after what had happened with his unit overseas. The man had been patient while Sean underwent treatment for PTSD. Mitch deserved to know where Sean was headed and why.

"Does this mean you've had a change of plans?" Mitch asked before Sean could explain himself.

"I'd like to see this case through," Sean said by way of explanation. "Considering I might have led a shooter right to her." He motioned toward the stairs. "Figured I'd take off once this wraps up."

Mitch gave a knowing nod. His boss was perceptive. Very little got past him, which made the predicament they were in even more surprising. Sean wasn't normally tailed without his knowledge, either.

"He got there first," Mitch pointed out. "At least, based on my understanding."

"Doesn't clear me of responsibility," Sean countered, feeling a punch in the center of his chest just thinking about it. Guilt infected every cell like a rogue virus unleashed on his system, killing every good thing in its path. The past threatened to drag him under. He took in a couple of slow, deep breaths, reminding himself there was no way to go back and change the past. This was exactly the reason he didn't do protection cases.

"You didn't sign up for this," Mitch stated. "No one would blame you for walking away. If anyone is responsible, it's me."

"We stick together, right?" Sean stated, figuring it was the best reassurance he could give under the circumstances. He and Mitch were stuck in a loop of trying to assuage the other's guilt. Both were stubborn, so neither would win. Mitch seemed to realize it, too. He half smiled as he nodded.

"See you in a few hours," Mitch said as Sean made his way out the door.

The ride back to Hamilton Pool Preserve gave Sean too much time inside his head. Being on the road with no distractions either cleared his mind or gave him way too much time to think. Tonight, overthinking was his curse. By the time he parked on the stretch of road closest to Raelynn's camping spot, a headache tried to split his head in two at the point right between his eyes.

It was black as pitch outside and the cold front that had been threatening was making good on its promise. The temperature had dropped fifteen degrees in the last half hour of his drive over and he felt the cooler temps to his bones as a light rain started to fall when he exited his vehicle.

Sean turned on the flashlight app on his phone, pointing the beam down to the ground as he pushed through the thick trees. If he was lucky, he'd make it to the campsite and back without getting his vehicle ticketed or towed. Austin was notorious for both, even though this area was out of the way and he should be fine. Locating the campsite in the dark would be impossible without night vision goggles. Thankfully, he kept a pair in his vehicle at all times.

Now that he was moving deeper into the thicket, he could switch to night vision. He turned off the phone app and then tucked his cell inside the front pocket of his jeans.

Methodically, he made his way through scrub brush as he listened for anything out of the ordinary. Experience said the shooter was long gone. No one had been arrested, though. Raelynn's campsite had been abandoned by her. The shooter might stick around to see if she came back to claim her belongings.

Branches slapped Sean in the face as the occasional raindrop pelted him on the cheek. The winds were picking up with each forward step as the thunder clapped overhead. Sean had faced worse conditions, although cold and wet were his least favorite. Being from Texas, the desert hadn't bothered him all that much. Dry heat was a bigger deal than folks realized. Humidity in Texas was on the rise every year.

Sean pulled out his cell phone to get his bearings. He'd mapped out the coordinates of where he believed the campsite should be located after jumping in the driver's seat back at headquarters. It also occurred to him that he needed to send a message to his brothers and sisters to let them know his trip home was delayed.

On second thought, he decided to wait until he knew when he might be making the trek. Checking his cell, he corrected his path slightly more to the east and then held it in his palm. He was getting close to where he guessed the site was and he probably should have thrown on a jacket considering a cold shiver raced down his spine. The tiny hairs on the back of his neck pricked. Those were the ones that warned him of danger.

Other than the chirp of crickets and various other insect sounds, he didn't hear anything that signaled a threat. Up ahead on the left, something moved. Zeroing in on the object, he realized it was a tent being whipped back and forth by the wind like a sailboat in an angry sea.

Now, he only hoped the guitar hadn't been stolen. There was no way he wanted to go back to Raelynn empty-handed, not after staring into those hazel eyes and seeing so much sadness there.

A twig snapped to his right. He turned his head and immediately saw movement low in the scrub brush. He squinted to get a better look. A porcupine methodically moved through the thicket, no doubt foraging for a meal. Sean had no problem leaving the animal to its mission. The trickle of rain was shifting, coming down at a steadier beat. If he didn't find the campsite soon, it might be too late to salvage the guitar.

Sean cursed underneath his breath. Much like the rain, the prickly feeling wasn't letting up. He surveyed the area one more time before deeming it safe to push forward. The top of the ground was slick with rain but the earth itself was parched. At this rate, he didn't have a huge threat of leaving tracks, especially if he got in and out.

The material being batted around by the wind turned out to be the tent he was looking for. Thankfully, the nylon and polyester material did a good job of protecting the case. He pulled up stakes and removed any signs Raelynn had camped there. She didn't need cops pinning her to the scene. If a record existed somewhere with her name on it, her stalker could confirm her location and use it to gain more information about her. There was no way Sean planned to make finding her any easier for the bastard by giving up her history. The guy would be able to compile information that would eventually allow him to make predictions about where she might end up next. Sean wasn't having it.

Wrapping up her belongings inside the tent would keep the rain off her essential items. He was taking all of it either way so she wouldn't leave a trail. As he circled back, lightning blazed across the sky. Out of the corner of his eye, he saw a dark lump.

Hell's bells. Sean was about to celebrate a win. Now, this night just got a whole lot worse. He recognized the shape. It was a body. And there was no movement, no breathing. Sean moved closer and squatted down. He stared at the person's back long enough to confirm he wasn't breathing.

Gunman? One of his victims?

Sean walked over and checked out the scene. There was definitely a dead body here. Male. The guy was face down, but he was wearing the same hoodie as the guy who'd been hunting Raelynn earlier. Since Sean hadn't gotten a good look at the perp's face, he had to make an educated guess this was the same person, given the clothing.

Seeing a dead body never got easier. His stomach churned as nausea tried to take hold, plant roots and send him spiraling into a pit of despair.

Sean made a mental note of the navy or black hoodie. He couldn't get a good read with the night vision goggles on. The hoodie was covering the guy's head, so assessing hair color was impossible without moving the body. He wouldn't make a mistake that could link him to a dead body. For now, he would assume this person was the shooter.

Rather than disturb a crime scene, or worse, leave his DNA here so his name became attached to an investigation, he started the trek back to his vehicle. Since he knew exactly where he was going, getting back to his vehicle didn't take long. The creepy feeling might have eased, but the real trouble was just beginning.

EVERY ONE OF Raelynn's song lyrics had to do with being on the run or being stalked. She scribbled down words here and there, managed to get out a few sentences, but nothing gelled into a song. She'd been able to write through heartache and loss, but a stalker left her mute on the page.

She exhaled, long and slow. She rubbed her temples to stave off the headache that had been threatening. And then she assessed whether or not she would be able to sleep if she tried. A hot shower had gone a long way toward calming her down. She tapped her pencil against the notepad sitting on her lap. A few deep breaths later, she wrote the word *father* in the center of the page. She circled the foreign word a couple of times.

A lot of time had passed since she'd wondered who her father might be; some might say ages had gone by. At this point, she couldn't remember the last time she'd thought about finding members of her family, let alone who they were. When she was young, she had had all the common fantasies that seemed to accompany being an orphan. For instance, she imagined her parents weren't dead but were instead abducted and would somehow find their way back to her. In another fantasy, they were being held hostage while holding on to a secret that involved national security. In yet another scenario, they were both spies who had had to distance themselves from her rather than risk putting her in danger.

All those ideas had died with her childhood, which had ended at the tender age of eleven as she'd watched her foster dad attack and nearly kill her foster mother. Their home was then deemed unfit, which had landed Raelynn back in the orphanage. The Nettles' home might not have been great, but it had been a step up from Sisters of Mercy, where Raelynn had been pushed up against walls in the hallway the second the nuns looked in the opposite direction. She'd been smacked, tripped and kicked. No one ever fessed up and the nuns didn't believe Raelynn despite the fact Hadley Arden sneered at her almost constantly. Hadley was popular with the others, who would also contribute to Raelynn's torture just to gain favor. The whole situation had been messed up, but it had taught Raelynn a lot about how group dynamics worked and whom she could trust.

Could she trust Mitch? The thought her father might have found her after all these years was still near impossible to process. She tapped her pencil on the notepad a little faster. Did she want to know if their DNA matched? Raelynn had gotten by just fine without parents until now. Why open that Pandora's box? What good would it do? She was no longer a child who cried herself to sleep every night hoping parents—essentially strangers—would magically show up, whisk her away and take her to a dream life where she lived in a castle and ponies ran wild. While she was at it, she should have asked for magical ponies that didn't bite. She'd never met a pony who didn't enjoy clamping his or her teeth down on her flesh when she least expected it.

Did she have a mother? Tap. Tap. Tap.

Of course, she had a mother. Biologically speaking, that was a given. But did she have a *mother*? Was there someone out there searching for Raelynn? Someone who lost sleep at night because she had no idea where her daughter was or if she was all right? Those thoughts would have haunted Raelynn if she'd given a baby up for adoption or had one taken away. More questions flooded her as she picked up the pace on the tapping.

Stomach acid churned. Bile burned the back of her throat.

And that's where she stopped herself.

Raelynn had been without both of her parents for almost thirty-one-years. The orphanage caretakers who were in charge said she'd been a colicky baby who cried for what ended up being the first six years of her life. Raelynn didn't have a lot of memories of herself before the age of ten. There were bits and pieces, almost like photographs instead of real remembrances. To be fair, she had most likely blocked most of them out a long time ago. But she remembered the helpless feeling in the pit of her chest, the hole in her heart that leaked what felt like battery acid.

Just thinking about finding her parents after all this time caused her hands to tremble. She squeezed the pencil to stop the tapping and broke it in half by accident. Families dredged up so many unwanted emotions. Raelynn didn't want to—no, *couldn't*—go back to that place in her mind where she was scared and alone.

In fact, she tossed the pencil and notepad on top of the nightstand to go find out if Sean was awake. Suddenly, she wanted to talk to him and maybe get his opinion on what she should do about Mitch and the DNA question.

A growing part of her wanted to leave well enough alone.

The hallway was dimly lit but she could see fine. Her room was the second one at the top of the stairs. She had a sneaky suspicion Sean's would be the first, considering how protective he'd been of her.

The wood flooring creaked as she stepped into the hallway—not exactly subtle. Then again, she'd seen the layers of security as they'd driven on to the property, at least the ones Mitch probably wanted strangers to be aware of as they entered his zone.

The door stood open and light emanated from the

space, but no sound came from the next room. Was Sean even there?

Raelynn tiptoed the rest of the way, only to find that Sean was gone. The emptiness in the pit of her stomach nearly caused her to double over. She wrapped her arm around her midsection in just enough time to stop herself from vomiting.

Anger replaced hurt. No one got to make her feel this out of control and helpless again. Not even Sean.

Chapter Six

Sean could hardly wait to run upstairs and deliver Raelynn's most prized possession. He hoped she was still awake so he could surprise her. Lights were on downstairs at the headquarters building, which meant Mitch was up late working. Could Sean slip past the boss and explain what he'd done later?

Raelynn's window faced the backyard, so he couldn't tell if she was still up from his parking spot out front. He untangled the guitar case from the tent lines after having to hastily toss everything inside and get out of the area. Hours had passed since he'd left to find her campsite. As much as he wanted to hand deliver the special instrument tonight, he would probably end up leaving it next to her door. She had to be worn out after the day she'd had. Any hope she might still be awake dwindled as he entered the code to unlock the door and then stepped inside.

Mitch's shirt was unbuttoned and his sleeves rolled up. He raked his hand through his hair after nodding toward Sean.

"Everything okay?" Sean asked as he heard himself ask the question. “Scratch that.” He made eye contact with Mitch. The man’s eyes were bloodshot from staring at a screen all night. “Do you want to talk about it?”

“What’s that?” Mitch asked, nodding toward the black case almost completely covered by stickers. His favorite was an oversize avocado wearing a Mexican hat while shaking maracas for reasons he couldn’t understand or explain. It tickled him.

“Belongs to our guest,” he responded, realizing Mitch seemed to pick up on the word *our*. “She left it at the campsite. Since it has a special meaning, I decided to go back and grab it for her before the rain did a number on it.”

Mitch’s eyebrow arched and his mouth opened to speak but it clamped shut almost as fast. Sean would have been sixteen or seventeen years old when Rae-lynn was born. It didn’t take a rocket scientist to figure out how that situation might have gone down. Sean couldn’t help but wonder if his boss had been aware of the pregnancy.

“I didn’t know,” Mitch said after a thoughtful pause, answering Sean’s biggest question. “Annalise…” He glanced up from the screen before studying it like it was a final exam and he was one credit shy of graduation. There was a whole load of shame in his eyes. “That’s her mother’s name.”

Sean nodded.

“She stopped returning my calls after our first time…”

Embarrassment turned Mitch’s cheeks four shades

past red. "I feel like I should have put it all together sooner."

"You know now," Sean stated, figuring it was better than never. "There isn't anything you can do to change the past."

A dark sense of amusement crossed Mitch's features. "There's no excuse. I had a child who grew up without parents. There's no letting myself off the hook when it comes to that."

Sean couldn't exactly disagree, and he'd come off as insincere if he tried. So, he didn't.

"I can't pretend to know what you're going through," Sean stated. "I'm certain that I'd be just as hard on myself if I was in the same position." That was a given. "I hope that someone like you or one of my coworkers would reassure me that I'd done everything possible to track down my child once I knew about him or her and—"

"That's the thing," Mitch interrupted. "I didn't. Once I suspected this might be the case, I pushed it all so far out of my mind that I tried to forget any of it existed." He leveled a gaze at Sean. "What does that make me?"

"Human," Sean stated.

"How so?" Mitch asked.

"For one, you weren't told there was a child for certain," Sean said.

"Shouldn't I have kept going until I found out one hundred percent for sure?" Mitch asked. His boss rarely ever showed signs of stress, let alone self-doubt. This was new territory for them both.

"Possibly," Sean hedged. "All I can say for certain is that I didn't know your circumstances, so it's impossible for me to make a determination about whether or not you were in the wrong. The situation sounds messed up to me. Your ex might have had her reasons for withholding information from you all those years ago. To your point, it's been three decades."

Mitch nodded. Sean was making headway.

"For all I know, I could have a kid out there somewhere and not know about it," Sean continued. "I've always been careful but you never know about these things. Nothing is a hundred percent."

"I was so busy licking my wounds all those years ago that it didn't occur to me that her family might be keeping us apart," Mitch continued. "She didn't have a say. Or, at least, that's what I'd like to believe."

"Why would she keep your child from you?" Sean asked, figuring that was the real question.

"Her parents," Mitch continued, not missing a beat, which meant it was the most honest answer. "They didn't like me. Said I was no good for her."

"And where is she now?" Sean continued, figuring a conversation with Annalise might be able to clear all of this up.

Mitch shook his head. Sean's heart sank at the implication.

"She's gone?" he asked.

"Last I heard," Mitch said with anguish written all over his face.

"I'm sorry, man," Sean stated with as much compassion as he could muster. "That's messed up." Her death meant there was no chance to go back and get closure. Annalise could clear up a lot of Mitch's questions. Now, he would have to rely on DNA to prove whether or not Raelynn was his daughter. She didn't seem like she was in any big hurry to swab the inside of her cheek or spit into a vial, whatever DNA collection method was used in these instances. He hadn't brought the subject up with her since they hadn't had a chance to talk. He had questions as to why she didn't seem eager to find answers.

Mitch drummed his fingers on the table.

"Thank you," he said. "Not much can be done about any of it now, except to right a wrong from a long time ago. I just wish I could have been there for her. She shouldn't have had to go through any of this with her parents or, even worse, alone." He rubbed the day-old scruff on his chin. "Hell, I don't know which would have been worse, to tell you the truth. Annalise's parents were the holier-than-thou types. If what I think is true, they would have crucified her for it." His hands fisted and Sean wasn't certain Mitch realized what he was doing. He seemed to catch on when he flexed and released his fingers like he was working off some of the tension.

"I'm sorry to hear it, man," Sean said, figuring there wasn't much else he could say. He meant it, though.

"I appreciate you," Mitch said. "I really do." He nodded toward the guitar. "Is that special to her? Is that what you said when you first came in?"

Sean nodded.

"Sorry to have pulled you off track," Mitch said with the kind of misery that made Sean's heart go out to the guy.

"Don't mention it," Sean said.

"What if she doesn't want to take the test?" Mitch asked in a desperate tone. "What if that ship has sailed for her and she doesn't want to know?"

"That's highly possible," Sean said, not wanting to offer false hope. "But you won't know until you give her time and let her come to it on her own."

"And if she doesn't come around?" Mitch asked, the torment visible in his eyes.

"Then you have to respect her wishes. Simple as that," Sean said, realizing it was easy to say, but not so easy to accept. There had been a pregnancy scare once when Sean was in his early twenties while on leave. He'd been too immature, too selfish to take care of himself let alone a family. Even though he'd always practiced safe sex, there was always that 2 percent chance contraception could fail.

Mitch nodded. He hadn't known about his child. Was it Raelynn? Would she give him the chance to find out?

EXHAUSTION FINALLY CLAIMED Raelynn as the sun was rising. Almost the minute she closed her eyes, it was time to open them again. She pushed up to sitting, ignoring the urge to curl up underneath the covers and go back to sleep for the rest of the day. How long had she been out, anyway?

A quick glance at the clock on the nightstand answered her question. Three hours was more like a nap, but she'd take it. Ever since leaving the tour, she'd slept in short bursts to keep moving. Staying in one place too long was dangerous. Real sleep, like a solid eight hours, was a luxury she couldn't afford.

The door to her bedroom was closed, so she couldn't hear activity from downstairs. Since it was after nine o'clock in the morning, she suspected the others were already awake and caffeinated. Speaking of which, she needed a cup of coffee to clear the cobwebs. A few hours of sleep here and there didn't exactly help with the brain power—precisely the reason someone had caught up to her. Granted, Sean was the best. He worked for an agency that employed ex-military. He found people or helped people disappear. Sometimes both, which gave her an idea.

After splashing cold water on her face in the adjacent bathroom, she threw on the warm-up outfit that had been folded and placed on the countertop in the bathroom with a note. This bathroom had three doors. There was the one that opened into her room, and another to an adjacent bedroom. The final one opened to the hallway. She didn't want to think about Sean sleeping in the adjacent room, not more than twenty feet away, so she forced her thoughts to brushing her teeth and how great it felt to be in a real home with a kitchen after camping the previous couple of nights.

The minute she stepped into the hall, her gaze dropped to the familiar case leaning against the wall where she would have to trip not to notice it. Her guitar? How? When?

She ran over to the case, dropped down to sitting on the beige carpeted floor and then crossed her legs. The familiar click of the snap-tight securing latches was music to her ears. Opening the case, seeing something so precious—something she believed might be lost forever—brought a flood of tears to her eyes. Successfully blinking them back, she picked up her favorite instrument and started strumming.

There was something raw and unfiltered about the sound of an acoustic guitar. It was music stripped back to its most basic form, and she loved it. As she strummed, words started coming to her… *Safe in your arms.* More bits of the song came to her as she figured out the refrain.

This was the magic she'd been searching for last night that couldn't be found with a notebook and a pencil. She needed to hear the notes being played. Raelynn reached for her cell phone and made a quick recording. The melody would play on repeat inside her head until more of the song took shape.

The smell of coffee wafted up the stairs. As far as days went, this one was off to a better start than any she could recall in recent history. Tucking her pick behind her ear, she kissed the strings before gently placing her guitar back in its case and putting it in her room.

Downstairs, Sean's masculine voice hit her before she made it into the kitchen. The low hum of conversation was oddly reassuring, and she couldn't wait to tell Sean how grateful she was for bringing her prized possession to her. He must have gone out in the rain last night to retrieve it.

She cleared her throat as she entered the room, not wanting to catch Sean or Mitch off guard. Surprising men with guns didn't seem like a smart move.

Sean's back was to her. He reached for a mug, stretching the cotton of his T-shirt over a strong back. But when he turned to face her, the real fireworks show began.

"Thank you," she said as her throat dried up. The words came out awkwardly, like she was back in high school, crushing on Brayden Wolff. He'd been the epitome of dark and brooding in tenth grade. *Detention* should have been his middle name. Wolff, as everyone had called him, was also a musician who'd dropped out by eleventh grade because school was "a waste of time" according to him. They'd been friends but nothing had ever developed beyond hanging out and talking about making a future in music. Just as feelings were starting to develop, they'd run out of time and he was gone. There'd been no last-minute goodbyes. Wolff had warned her it was the only way he could go. Once he knew it was time, he had to move on and not look back. No regrets.

She thought about him from time to time, wondered what he was doing. Since he wasn't exactly on social media, she'd lost track of where he'd gone, until one day curiosity got the best of her. After a little research, she'd learned the young person they'd all called Wolff was a potbellied truck driver for a major retail chain. No music. No tours like he'd dreamed. Just three kids between two exes and a job the same as his stepfather, a man he'd despised.

Raelynn was proud of her accomplishments, which made it that much more difficult to turn her back on her hard-fought career.

"You're welcome," Sean said, like it was the most natural thing for someone to do something so incredible for her. "But it was the least I could do."

She opened her mouth to argue, then clamped it shut. One of her best attributes was knowing when she would lose an argument. To a person like Sean, going out of his way to perform a random act of kindness probably was an everyday affair. To her, his actions meant the world.

"Coffee?" he asked as she glanced at Mitch out of the corner of her eye. His serious expression told her more was going on than establishing paternity.

"Yes, but I can get it myself," she offered.

"I'm already here," he said. His rebuttal came as fast as a mood change. "Cream? Sugar?"

"No, thanks," she said, preferring nothing got in the way of a strong cup of fresh brew. Besides, she couldn't tell if the coffee was any good or not once it had all those extras.

She took the offering being handed to her. One look in Sean's eyes and she steadied herself for the news about to be delivered.

"When I went to your camping site…" he began,

searching her eyes before continuing. He must have been satisfied she could handle the news because he added, "…there was a body."

Chapter Seven

Sean searched Raelynn's eyes, watching the panic as it unfolded while feeling helpless as hell to stop her pain. For a split second, he flashed back to Kandahar and the incident that had caused his hands to tremor to this day. Shaking off the mental image before it could take hold, he refocused on Raelynn.

"What happened?" she asked as she seemed to be catching her breath.

"There aren't a lot of details so far," he stated. "I called in an anonymous tip about a smell in the area. Said I didn't get close enough to investigate because I thought there might have been a wild animal encounter involved. And then I ended the call."

"Won't they be able to trace your number?" she asked.

He shook his head, not going into the technical details of how the call would be bounced off a different cell tower than the one close to him. Plus, his cell was encrypted.

"Oh," she said before taking a sip of coffee. She white-knuckled the mug with both hands at this point. Her breathing was fast and shallow. All the physical signs of being under duress were there.

When she dropped her left hand, he reached for it. Physical contact had a way of grounding people. Then he looked into her eyes, catching her gaze and holding on to it. Hearing about death was never easy. Being close to death was never easy. Watching death was…

He couldn't go there right now. Raelynn needed compassion more than he needed to beat himself up over past mistakes.

The moment was so charged that the second their hands touched, though, fireworks went off in his chest. Their gazes broke off and she pulled her hand back, then excused herself before running out the door. Mitch's voice was background noise as Sean went after her. She needed to know that he hadn't meant to overstep any bounds.

Not two feet outside the door, she spun around to face him.

"I didn't mean…" Those hazel eyes of hers pleaded for him to understand.

"Don't think twice about it," he reassured. "I'm here to apologize and make sure we're okay."

"Okay?" she asked with disappointment in her voice that sent a mixed signal. "I don't want to be just okay."

Before he could respond, she took a step toward him and brought her hands up to hold on to his shoulders as though hanging on for life. And then she pressed up to her tiptoes and kissed him. The second those pink lips touched his, a bomb detonated and warning sirens wailed.

Grasping at every ounce of self-discipline, he pulled back.

"Not a good idea," he said.

Her eyebrows drew together and then her cheeks turned four shades of pink. "I'm sorry. I must have misread the..."

"No, you didn't," he said, stopping her before she could really get going on that sentence and the self-doubt that would accompany it. "You read me spot-on."

"Then, I'm confused," she stated.

"You've been through a lot lately. You just heard about a dead person next to where you set up camp. Those things combined do strange things to the mind and you were most likely reaching out for comfort," he explained, hoping he was doing it justice.

"That's what you think just happened?" she asked, but it came across as more statement than question. Shaking her head, she mumbled something he couldn't quite catch and knew better than to ask her to repeat based on her tone. Before he could settle on a question, she brushed past him and walked back inside.

Sean stood there for a long moment, trying to decide what had just happened. His original belief that emotions had gotten the best of Raelynn and she was only looking for proof of life in the kiss didn't seem to be holding ground. He knew exactly where his mind was. His heart betrayed logical thinking by wanting more. The situation with Raelynn was a powder keg, especially considering she might be the daughter of his boss. Mitch had been nothing but kind to Sean when he'd needed a hand up. No matter how right being with Raelynn felt in the moment, Sean couldn't let emotion override rational thought. He wouldn't do that to Mitch or to Raelynn while so much in her life was in chaos. As much as his ego wanted to believe she wanted him, he needed to know it was the real deal.

Whoa. Where did that come from all of a sudden? Since when did he need to be certain a woman wasn't using him to keep her feet on the ground?

A chuckle rolled up and out, even though, technically, nothing was funny. After a deep breath, he turned and headed back inside.

The air inside the room was tense. Mitch was still at his laptop, searching for answers. He'd made a couple of calls last night to find out the identity of the dead body. Those last two words sat heavy on his chest. There'd been too much death in his life.

Since Raelynn's back was to him and she didn't turn around when he walked inside, he figured he was the last person she wanted to see right now.

"What did you find out so far?" he asked Mitch, heading toward his boss's desk.

Raelynn moved around the kitchen, shutting cabinets a little loudly as she hunted around for food and cooking supplies. Sean probably should kick himself for ruining a relationship before it had a chance to get off the ground. *Relationship* might be a strong word. He'd settle for anything right now, considering how badly he'd just blown it. Rather than get inside his head searching for the real reason he'd pushed her away, he sat on the corner of Mitch's desk and folded his arms across his chest.

"On the campsite situation, not much," Mitch admitted. When he didn't sleep, it showed in the bags cradling his eyes.

"What about digging into who set us up to find Raelynn?" Sean continued.

"I didn't get much further there," Mitch said without looking up.

"Drake Johnson could be responsible," Sean said. "Things between the two of you have been heating up lately. Maybe he decided to make this a personal attack."

Mitch rubbed the scruff on his chin.

"Anything's possible at this point," he said on a frustrated sigh. "The person who contacted me seems to have gone missing."

"I know we don't normally discuss these details but throw out a name in case Raelynn recognizes it," Sean requested.

"Good point," Mitch said as Raelynn froze in front of the stove where she was throwing together scrambled eggs.

It wouldn't hurt for Sean to hear the name, too, just in case he could make a connection neither one of them could.

"We're looking for someone by the name of Jason Quick," Mitch explained. "Does that ring any bells?"

Raelynn barely turned when she shook her head.

"He supposedly works for an oil company and said he was searching for a half sister. He gave the name of the orphanage where you grew up and said you had red hair," Mitch said. "He contracted us under the guise of his father offering a deathbed confession of an illegitimate child who was also an heir. Apparently, there's no inheritance if Quick doesn't find his sister."

Sean wanted to ask how those details ended up causing Mitch to come to the conclusion Raelynn could be his child. Right now didn't seem like the right moment.

"This 'sister' turning up dead sure would be a good reason not to have to share the inheritance," Sean reasoned. Greed was one of the top motives for murder.

"I couldn't agree more," Mitch said. "Which was also the reason I had my colleague verify the details."

"Hold on a second," Raelynn said, leaning her slender hip against the counter after turning off the stove. "When I was on tour, any random person could have gotten off a shot. Why not just be done with it?"

"I'm just throwing out ideas here to see if any of them stick, but that would seem a little too obvious," Sean interjected.

"The stalker sends me into hiding and then… what? What's the endgame?" she said. "I don't understand how an obsessed fan could be linked with the case you've been put on."

"Police are looking for a stalker who has escalated. It might be a decoy," Sean concluded. It was as simple as that.

"And what about you guys?" she asked.

"Apparently, you're better at hiding than Quick anticipated," Mitch said.

"It's one hypothetical, but there are other possibilities," Sean pointed out—too many to settle on the first one that had teeth to it. "Jason Quick might be a false identity."

"TIME WILL TELL," Mitch seemed to agree. "It's a place to start."

Raelynn shifted her weight to the right, overcorrected, then took a step to stop from falling over. Unfortunately, her elbow flew forward. She caught the tip on the pan, burning the hell out of her skin. "Ouch."

At least she caught the handle of the pan before eggs ended up splattered all over the tile floor, cabinets and ceiling. She sucked in a breath before returning the pan to a back burner this time. "Close call."

Sean was at her side, ready to scoop up anything before it hit the floor. "You got it?"

"Yes," she said quietly. His male presence beside her, filling her senses with his spicy and clean scent, wasn't doing great things to an already overactive pulse. "Thanks."

"No problem," he said, like being on the ready and by her side in two seconds flat was normal.

Raelynn sighed. The kiss from a little while ago was still burned into her lips no matter how much she tried to refocus. Her lips seemed to have a memory of their own and weren't afraid to cancel out logic. Logic said Sean wasn't attracted to her, despite the chemistry she felt crackling between them. She blamed it for causing her to act on instinct when she should have employed at least a few of her brain cells to stop herself. Impulse control wasn't normally an issue for her, so she was scratching her head as to why it seemed to be now.

Did she need a distraction? Proof that she was still in control of her life? Those seemed to be Sean's conclusions. Every molecule in her body screamed the opposite. Raelynn had always known what she wanted. She could only assume Sean was politely rejecting her.

He didn't make eye contact when he retrieved a plate and handed it over. Instead, he moved back to the desk corner and reclaimed his seat after pouring a fresh cup of coffee.

"Where were we?" he asked Mitch as she plated her scrambled eggs.

Too hungry to take time to toast bread, she grabbed a couple of slices and then a bottle of ketchup from the fridge. Sitting down at the breakfast bar, she assembled her egg sandwich. Eating it didn't take long and she relished every bite after living off power bars and fruit when she could get ahold of it. Nothing had been cooked in a long time, especially not while camping over the last two nights near Hamilton Pool Preserve. She'd been making the rounds at various campsites recently, and this one had seemed like a good idea despite restrictions against it. Her thoughts shifted to a human being murdered over finding her. An involuntary shiver rocked her body.

"Coming up with motive for murder," Mitch stated as his gaze shifted toward her. He must have seen her reaction out of the corner of his eye. "Everything all right over there?"

"As much as it can be under the circumstances," she offered. She was still trying to add up why someone would possibly pretend to stalk her before murdering her. Then again, maybe the stalker made for an easy cover. "The person who hired you might not turn out to be real. He might be a front or a cover."

Mitch nodded. She examined his features. He had the same color eyes as her and a reddish tint to his dark hair. Could be from the sun, though. It didn't necessarily mean that he was her father. She looked for other signs they might be related.

Raelynn stopped herself. There was a quick and easy way to find out if Mitch was her father. The DNA test sat on the other side of his monitor. He'd dropped the subject, which she appreciated. Was he letting her come into her own about the decision whether or not to take the test without any extra pressure from him?

The man must want to know the results. Was it possible he'd been low-key searching for her for a while now despite telling her the opposite? As much as she wanted to ask how she crossed over into his own investigation, she didn't want to open a can of worms. He deserved an answer so he could either keep going in his search or know to stop. She wouldn't hold out forever, just until she knew how she felt about the possibility of being found by a parent after all these years. She'd put the issue to rest in her mind long ago. Dredging it up again made her feel like that same little girl who'd cried herself to sleep most nights.

Sadness and despair roiled in the pit of her stomach for the scared and lonely kid she used to be. Was she ready to face her past?

The short answer was not right this second. Before this investigation was over, she resolved to take the test for Mitch's sake. She might offer the sample and then walk out the door before the result came in. Either way, he deserved the information.

Mitch's cell buzzed, breaking into her heavy thoughts. As he answered it, he stood up and took a walk outside, leaving her alone with Sean once again. Should she say something to ease the awkwardness between them?

"More coffee?" she asked for lack of a good starting place.

He picked up his cup and then tilted it before taking a sip from the mug with a glowing sun on the side. "I forgot about this one."

"It's probably cold by now," she said as he made a face. "I can top it off to warm it up if you'd like."

The right words weren't coming, so she started to chicken out of bringing up the topic of the kiss at all.

"I can do it," he said, pushing up to standing before walking over near where she sat on the stool at the breakfast bar.

"It's no trouble," she said. She'd never been good at conversation. Sitting down and writing out her words in the form of a song had always been her preferred method. Then again, her process didn't make for good relationships. She wasn't *good* at those.

As she gathered up her courage to apologize and try to clear the air between them, the door opened and Mitch walked in. Tension lines slashed his forehead and his mouth formed a thin line.

"The body found by Raelynn's campsite has been identified as Jason Quick," he said as her heart sank. Knowing someone had been killed before had been awful, the worst. Having a name, one they'd just been discussing, made everything so much more real. And this nightmare seemed to have no end.

"This makes no sense," Mitch said. "I was hired by Jason Quick to find a person by the name of Raelynn at the same time I'm getting information that I might have a daughter from a mystery person. How does this information intersect?"

"Now the guy who hired you is dead," Sean surmised. "Are we supposed to think this is all one big coincidence? Does someone think we'll stop looking now?"

"Or did they kill Jason Quick to keep him from talking?" Mitch asked.

"I have a question on a different topic," Raelynn jumped in after a thoughtful pause. "Why would the woman you believe is my mother give me up in the first place? Why wouldn't she tell you about me?"

"Her parents were religious," Mitch explained. "There's no way she would go to them with this information. If she told me, I would never have given you…*the baby* up." He flashed an apology for the slip of familiarity.

Someone died because of this mess. Did Mitch have information that could clear this up. Or was Jason Quick the last person who had any answers?

Chapter Eight

"How did it happen? The murder?" Sean asked as Mitch moved to the breakfast island and took a seat on a stool. He half sat on the leather material, kicking his foot back to rest on the metal.

"I don't have much in the way of details from the law," Mitch admitted.

"Any chance we can request access to the coroner's report?" Sean continued.

"Done," Mitch said. He picked up his cell phone and fired off a text. "I was already planning to pull a few strings."

"Jason Quick is a real person?" Raelynn said the words quietly, her voice revealing her not-so-mild state of shock at the news.

"It seems so," Mitch stated.

"The question is whether or not he is the person he pretended to be," Sean said, figuring Quick might have been a sacrificial lamb. The fact he was the one who'd inquired about Raelynn and had hired them to find her wasn't information to be ignored. It was a little too easy for the person who'd inquired about

Raelynn to be dead. Or was it? Sometimes the simple answer was the right one.

"And it's a good question at that," Mitch said.

The morning had evaporated at this point. It was time for lunch, even though he wondered if anyone could eat. Raelynn had gotten up the latest. She'd just eaten. Mitch should probably eat, but knowing him, he wouldn't be able to. Sean was on his third cup of coffee and there were very few answers as to what had really happened or what the true threat really was. The law would need at least a little bit of time to investigate. Mitch would be able to get ahold of much of the information through his network. What couldn't be obtained legally could be otherwise retrieved using whatever means necessary as long as it wasn't illegal. The same rules that applied to law enforcement officers didn't necessarily apply to their organization since they weren't exactly building court cases here. Their job involved using whatever avenues they had to in order to get the job done.

Raelynn sat there, quiet—almost eerily quiet. He was starting to be very concerned about her. Shock seemed to be taking hold again, and he had to fight every protective instinct inside him before he headed over to her and hauled her against his chest to bring her comfort. The kiss from earlier kept finding its way back front and center in his thoughts. Keep this up and he'd be in real trouble.

"How do they know for certain it's Jason Quick?" Raelynn finally asked.

"There was ID on the body that matched his description," Mitch stated.

"It's possible the ID is fake," Sean interjected. "We need to do some investigating on our own to verify the facts. We won't take anything for granted and we sure as hell won't make any decisions based on data that we don't know is one-hundred-percent reliable."

"Okay," she said with a little more confidence in her voice this time. "What's our next step? Is there anything we can do now to get the wheels moving?"

He could already see them churning in her mind. He had to give credit where credit was due—she was holding it together well considering all that had been going on. Thinking about her as an orphan made him realize she was probably strong because of the struggles she'd had growing up. He knew a little bit about fighting his way through life. And yet she had experienced more challenges than any young person should have to face.

"Right now, we continue to investigate from here at home base," he said. "Going out while everything is still hot could prove a fatal mistake. We have no idea about the conditions under which Jason Quick was killed or why. Since we know so little, it would be irresponsible to bring you out in public."

Those words seemed to hit like harpoons straight to her chest.

Whoever was after her most likely still was. Sean had a bad feeling Jason Quick's death was a warning sign more than anything else. There was no reason to believe any of this would stop now that Quick was gone.

"If no one needs me, I think I'll head upstairs for a little while," Raelynn said. The dark circles underneath her eyes matched Mitch's. When Sean really thought about it, there were a few more similarities between her and his boss, all of which had to be weighing heavily on her mind. She had to notice how much the two of them favored each other and he wondered if she'd made any decisions about DNA testing.

"Go ahead," Mitch said before Sean had a chance to respond. He would have said the same thing. In fact, he owed her an apology, so he followed her.

Raelynn didn't stop until she reached the top of the stairs. When she turned around to face him, she was right at eye level.

Bringing her hand up to his chest, she stopped him flat-out. A warning issued from her intense gaze.

"It's okay," she said to him with a look that made him realize how much he'd hurt her with his earlier actions. At this point, there was no hope in getting her to trust him again. An apology was still necessary.

Sean stood on the step. "I wanted to clarify something from earlier this morning."

Raelynn brought her hand back, crossing her arms over her chest. There was a detachment in her eyes now that made him miss the fiery spark.

"That kiss was probably the best thing that's happened to me all year, maybe longer, and I wanted you to do it because you wanted to kiss me and not because you were having a reaction to being in danger," he said. The admission left him feeling more vulnerable than ever before.

Raelynn crossed her arms over her chest. Her body language said she wanted nothing to do with him. The sudden chill in the air said she was done with this conversation. And yet, when her tongue slicked across her bottom lip, she faltered.

"I'm sorry for hurting you," he said softly. "That wasn't my intention at all."

Her stare spoke volumes, even while her lips remained clamped shut.

"There hasn't been anyone in my life in a very long time who made me want to reexamine my life choices and be a better person until you," he said honestly. "Since you'd been through one hell of an experience, I needed to make sure what was happening was genuine. I *wanted* it to be real and not some knee-jerk reaction to the worst day of your life."

RAELYNN STUDIED HIM CLOSELY, trying to evaluate just how much this guy could hurt her. Letting people in wasn't exactly her forte. Arm's distance had always been a comfortable length. Give an inch and she risked more than she needed to under the circumstances. Before long, she'd be on the road again, either moving on undercover or back with the tour. She hoped it would be the latter of the two for many reasons.

After a moment to gather her thoughts, she said,

"I accept your apology but that doesn't mean I'd be willing to go down that road again. You've done a whole lot for me in a short time, and I appreciate it. Kissing you out of the blue like I did overstepped a boundary that shouldn't have been crossed. Whether we were both willing doesn't matter in the grand scheme of things."

A wall came up between them so fast Raelynn's head was almost spinning. Turned out she wasn't the only one who knew how to take a step back from people.

Sean leaned against the wall.

"During my tour overseas, there was this little kid," he started, staring at the opposite wall like he was unable to make eye contact. "I say he was a little kid. In reality, he might have been around twelve years old, give or take. He didn't seem to have a family since locals usually handed him scraps of food when he showed up."

A look crossed his features as he recalled the memory—a memory that seemed certain to take him to a painful place inside himself based on the way he appeared to close up.

"No one seemed to know where this kid came from or where he went when he disappeared," Sean continued. "He would sell bottles of water to soldiers."

"I'm guessing you all took pity on him and bought out his supply," she surmised.

Sean nodded.

"This went on for weeks while we were stationed

in the village. This place was a haven for women and children. We were there to guard them," he said.

Raelynn took in a long slow breath as Sean paused. She had a bad feeling this story was about to go south.

"Word came that we had to clear out. The Taliban were headed our way and we were assigned to get as many locals out as possible. The problem with the kid was that he wasn't from this particular village, so we couldn't take him," Sean said.

"Oh, no. I'm so sorry," Raelynn said, holding back tears that pricked the backs of her eyes. They were always there, ready, and yet so difficult to let fall. It was almost like there was an invisible wall they could never penetrate, a barrier that held them back no matter how much they continued to build and pressure the barricade.

"It's worse than that," Sean said, so low she almost couldn't hear him.

Instinctively, she reached out for his hand, grateful he didn't pull away when they made contact. Electricity pulsed through her hand and up her arm, bringing awareness to every place it touched.

"Last minute, I let him sneak onto the back of our convoy," he said, leaning his head back against the wall and closing his eyes. "He had a bomb strapped to his chest that day and I lost my best friends. Their deaths were on me."

"You couldn't have known that would happen," Raelynn immediately defended with conviction. He needed to hear those words until he believed them.

"Their blood is on my hands," he countered. The tremors in his returned.

"I can't pretend to know what that feels like, so I won't try," she said, fighting back an onslaught of emotions trying to shatter the impenetrable force field. She'd become so good at combatting her feelings, which was probably the reason they couldn't penetrate the barrier. "And I won't try to convince you that I'm an expert on anything to do with you because we've only just met."

She searched for a reaction, but he was so still, so blank, that she couldn't read him.

"What you've done for me in the short time I've known you is nothing short of a miracle. No one, and I mean no one, has ever gone out of their way, let alone put their life on the line," she said, hoping she could ease some of the burden of guilt that was written all over his body language.

"I was doing my job," he said almost robotically.

"Would you have gone back to find my campsite so you could bring me this if that was true?" she asked, motioning toward her guitar.

Sean issued a sharp sigh.

"No," he admitted.

"It's just who you are," she said. "You care about helping someone out when they've all but lost hope."

"And yet I still murdered my friends," he said in that detached voice from a moment ago.

"Awful people were responsible for the deaths of your friends," she corrected. "You no more did that than I killed Jason Quick, even though part of me feels like he wouldn't be dead if it wasn't for me."

"Don't do that to yourself," Sean said, bringing his free hand up to his forehead like he was trying to push back a headache. He didn't open his eyes and he suddenly sounded exhausted.

He might not be willing to give himself a break, but she suspected he would do almost anything to make her feel better. She decided to throw in a request and see what happened.

"Would you lie down with me for a little while?" she asked, going for it. At the very least, they would both get in a little rest. "There isn't much we can do while we wait for information, and I've been surviving on two- and three-hour bursts of sleep for weeks now. It's about that time for me to grab some shut-eye and I could use the company."

He didn't immediately speak.

"In fact," she hedged, "I might actually be able to get real sleep if there's someone else in the room." She was betting on his generosity. He looked tired but she figured he would push through if there wasn't an excuse to slow down.

Sean nodded, released her hand and then pushed himself upright. He immediately offered a hand. She took the offering. This time, she wasn't caught off guard by the electrical impulses shooting up her arm. This time, she welcomed them.

He toed off his boots at the door and shrugged out of his T-shirt before joining her on the bed. He didn't make a move or try to climb underneath the sheets. Raelynn excused herself to change into yoga pants and a T-shirt from the pile he brought back from her campsite. She had a better chance of getting real sleep if she was comfortable. Since it would take time to get information back about the murder investigation, rest now was the best move. Once the intel started flooding them, she had a feeling they would be on the go.

Besides, she couldn't stay here forever, even if it was the first time she felt safe.

After switching clothes, she stepped into the bedroom. Her heart skipped a beat when she saw a shirtless Sean stretched out on top of the covers. His hands were clasped behind his head, drawing even more attention to a stomach that was nothing but ripples upon ripples of muscled perfection. Clearly, the man had a workout routine that was working for him.

"Mind if I close the blinds?" she asked.

"Be my guest," he responded. His deep timbre washed over her, making her wish the kiss didn't have to be the last one. It did, though. There was no changing the fact.

Raelynn walked to the pair of windows before twisting the rod that closed the blinds. She pulled blackout curtains shut, as well. The room was nice, clean. It was efficient. There was a bed, a small dresser and a pair of nightstands. A wingback chair sat in the corner of the room. One of the nightstands had a clock on it and the other had a lamp. There was a docking station with what looked like every conceivable outlet on it meant to charge devices. This place was made for folks who needed to grab sleep at any time of day or night.

Since it was pitch-black in the room, Raelynn felt her way over to the bed. Her hand landed on Sean's strong arm.

"Sorry," she whispered.

"Honest mistake," he concluded. But then he tugged her onto the bed, and she could hear him scooting over—not that she needed to rely on her ears, because she could feel his presence as he shifted. His masculine scent was everywhere on the sheets and pillowcase, and all she could do was surrender to feeling him surround her.

Raelynn curled up on her side, not wanting to risk tempting herself again being so close to Sean. Then he tugged her toward him before wrapping his arm around her. Her first thought was that she could stay like this forever. The second her heart stopped racing, she closed her eyes and fell asleep.

A noise caused Raelynn to bolt upright. It was still black as pitch inside the room and it took a few seconds for her to orient herself. On instinct, her hand reached toward the side of the bed where Sean had been sleeping next to her.

The bed was cold. For a split second, she thought she might have dreamt Sean was here at all. Then, she heard his muffled voice drifting up from downstairs, and she realized how much she missed him.

Chapter Nine

"What time is it?" Raelynn asked as she stepped into the kitchen. Her hair was slicked back in a ponytail, fresh from the shower.

"Four o'clock," Sean said. He'd slept for a straight eight. He'd gotten up around nine last night and had been awake ever since.

"I thought the clock upstairs stopped working," she said with a yawn as she stretched. The cotton fabric pulled taut against her full breasts. The feel of her wrapped around his left side was stamped in his thoughts. "It felt like I slept a whole lot longer than a couple of hours."

"We went to bed yesterday," he supplied, much to her shock. The way her mouth formed an argument that never materialized made him think about how incredible those lips had felt when they'd been pressed against his own. No doubt she got attention for her looks, but talking to her and getting to know her made his heart want to open up, even if just a little. Sharing his past wasn't something he'd done with anyone else. With Raelynn, speaking the words out loud chipped away at his guard.

"What?" she asked, looking like she needed a few seconds for the information to sink in. She glanced around as though trying to get her bearings. "I thought I heard voices down here. Where's Mitch?"

"Are you sure about that? I'm the only one here but I was on the phone a minute ago," he offered. The details of the call weren't something he could discuss since it was classified information—not to mention, her knowing wouldn't help her current situation or change a thing.

"I guess that's right," she said. "I distinctly heard your voice. Maybe no one else." She took a slow breath as her gaze dropped to the ring finger on his left hand. She seemed relieved when there was no gold band, but it was possible he was seeing what he wanted to, instead of what was there.

"Then it was probably just me," he confirmed as he realized he'd never answered her other question. "Mitch will be back in about an hour. He had to run out for another case."

She nodded as her gaze shifted to the fridge behind him.

"You were out a long time, so you must be starving," he realized.

"I could eat," she said as her hand went to her stomach.

"Let's see what we can dig up," he said as he moved to the fridge, then started pulling out supplies. "Are you hungry for breakfast, lunch or dinner?"

"I'd take anything at this point as long as it's fast," she said with a smile—a smile that sent more of that warmth spiraling through him. Her soft skin against his body had nearly undone him while they were in bed together. Her steady, even breathing had signaled she'd fallen asleep almost as fast as her eyes must have closed. Surprisingly, he'd crashed for hours and woke up to her curled around his left side. The smell of citrusy shampoo was still imprinted in his brain. He would never look at lemons or limes in the same way again.

"The fruit in the bowl is ready to eat," he said, motioning toward the counter. Next, he pulled out lunch meat along with enough ingredients to make a decent sandwich. By the time he'd assembled one, she'd polished off an apple and was making a fresh pot of coffee.

The sandwich disappeared before the drip ended its cycle.

"Is that enough food?" he asked. "Because I can make more."

"No, that was perfection," she said, shaking her head. He probably didn't need to focus on the way her actions caused citrus to fill the air. He must have made a face because she immediately asked, "What just happened?"

Saying "You" was probably not an ideal response. He decided to go for "Nothing." And then he made a move for the kitchen cabinet to find a pair of coffee mugs, figuring coffee was as good a distraction as anything. He filled the cups before handing one over. Once again, he was caught off guard by the reaction his body had toward their fingers grazing.

She blew on the rim before taking a sip.

"I've decided to take the DNA test," she said.

"Mitch will be thrilled," Sean acknowledged.

"Maybe not. There's a catch," she warned.

"Which is?" he asked.

"I don't want to know the results," she admitted.

"Can I ask why?" he continued.

"What would be the point?" she asked on a shrug. "I'm an adult. I'm raised. Reared. Whatever you want to call it. The point is, I'm beyond needing to be parented, even though I understand that Mitch probably needs confirmation as to whether or not he needs to keep searching for his daughter." She took another sip of coffee. "I don't want to be the reason he can't sleep at night because he's wondering if the search is over."

"That's pretty selfless of you," Sean said, "especially since you don't want anything in return." There were plenty of people out there who would take one look at the operation Mitch had started and want to figure out a way to get their hands on a piece of it. Raelynn wasn't that kind of person. Sean had noticed early on that she seemed ready to put in the work for any successes she had. Her willingness to give Mitch closure, even at a personal cost to herself, didn't go unnoticed. Would she truly be able to walk away, though?

"It's the least I can do after all the things both of you are doing to help me," she stated. "There's a decent chance that we won't be a match. He needs to be free so he can keep searching."

"Mitch won't forget the gesture," he said. His boss didn't take this kind of thing lightly. He was in the business of helping others get closure. Sean was just realizing how awful it must be for Mitch not to have it in his own personal life.

"I'm not looking for anything from him," she said, as though he needed clarification. "It occurred to me that everyone deserves a chance to know they had a kid. As great of a person he seems to be, I don't need him."

"You already said that," Sean said, figuring it was a sign she needed people more than she wanted to let on, or possibly even admit to herself. He, of all people, understood where she was coming from. He'd spent the better part of his life convincing himself that he didn't need anyone else. Living on the ranch had been a nightmare after his father died while Sean was still a kid. The main person responsible for Sean's frustration, Duncan Hayes, hadn't been the nurturing type. He'd stepped in as a male role model after Sean's father died, but Duncan had ended up pushing Sean and his siblings away from the family business in their hometown of Cider Creek and their home by being a rigid son of a bitch. But he didn't want to get into that right now.

"So I did," she said, as though she was just realizing he was right. "Sorry. The caffeine hasn't kicked in yet."

"All you need is—" he checked his watch "—eighteen more minutes for that to happen."

Her eyebrow shot up.

"It takes twenty minutes for caffeine to kick in," he clarified.

"Anything new on the investigation into Jason Quick's murder?" she asked, moving to the stool at the breakfast bar. She half sat, half leaned against it.

"Turns out his real name is Anton Miles, not Jason Quick," Sean reported. "Does that name ring any bells?"

She shook her head.

"He's a tech worker," Sean said. "Mitch put out feelers and the information checked out."

"What on earth would a tech worker want with me?" she asked with an incredulous quality to her tone.

"It doesn't make sense to us yet, either," he said. "But it will."

Given enough time, they could figure out anything. As long as time didn't run out for Raelynn before they found answers, they'd be okay.

"THE CAFFEINE MIGHT be kicking in early, or maybe I've just finally had some sleep," Raelynn began. "We should probably take a look at any connections Anton Miles might have to my road crew."

"Good idea," Sean said, and she tried not to let his voice penetrate the wall she had to keep up between them. The barrier was as much for his own good as it was for hers. "Can I ask what drew you to your line of work in the first place?"

"I like writing songs and other people wouldn't sing them the way I heard them inside my head, so

I decided to do it myself," she said. Would she be happier at home with a small studio recording songs instead of on the road for weeks on end? The short answer was a resounding yes.

"Do you like singing?" he asked.

"In the shower. Around the house. In a recording studio. Just not in front of a live audience," she admitted. "Being on stage terrifies me. But then I get going on a set and my nerves calm down. Suddenly, I'm into the music and able to forget all the background noise. When I get in that headspace, it's pure magic."

"Does it happen every time?" he asked.

"Almost," she said. "Since I picked up a stalker, though, it's been near impossible. Every time I look out onto the crowd, I wonder if he's out there and I'm miserable."

"What about a bodyguard?" he asked.

"I mean, sure, when you hit it big and can afford one," she explained. "At the stage my career is… I pretty much have to manage everything on a shoestring budget. There isn't much left for personal security."

"Don't you tour with bigger names?" he asked.

"Yes," she said. "As long as I'm with them, I'm generally pretty safe. The problem is their security isn't getting paid to babysit me. If I go to the grocery store or run to the bank, I'm on my own."

"What about your road crew? How close are you to them?" he asked.

"Rudy Cannon has been my stage manager for

a couple of years now," she said. "His cousin Mark used to set up for me. When it came time for him to stay home with his wife while she was pregnant and on bed rest, he recommended his cousin."

"How is Rudy at his job?" he asked.

"Honestly?" she asked, but it was a rhetorical question. "He did better in the beginning. This past year he's had some issues with gambling. There are times when I have to go find him at the track when he's supposed to be setting up."

"Have you had a lot of disagreements? Fights?" he asked.

"If you're asking if I've chewed him out, the answer is yes," she said. "I'm not proud of the fact that I've lost my temper. I have, though. My nerves are already on edge at the reality of going on stage. Having unreliable help doesn't exactly offer a lot of reasons to be calm."

"What's his response?" Sean continued.

"He doesn't like it," she said. "There is an understanding between us that he'll show up on time and get his work done. I'm the one who has to hold him accountable to his word. When I have to track him down, it can get heated between us. It always blows over, though."

"If a stalker stops you from working, he doesn't get paid," Sean reasoned. "It doesn't make sense that he would want to lose his income."

"Gambling doesn't make sense to me, either," she said. "He's not stupid. Though, he does make bad choices sometimes."

"Bad how? Other than being late to work and gambling?" he asked.

"Women, for one," she said. "He's given out backstage passes that he had no business handing out."

"Is there any chance someone's husband blames you for his wife cheating?" he asked.

"And decided to come after me?" Hearing the words out loud make her think it wasn't likely. She shook her head.

"Who else is in your world?" he asked.

"Erik and Ashley Bradshaw are sponsoring me," she said.

"Isn't he a real estate developer in Dallas?" he asked.

"Yes, that's the one," she stated. "I've been their pet project."

"How do they feel about you being off the road right now?" he asked.

"Not good," she said. "They're losing money on their investment in me if I can't hop back on the tour."

"Doesn't make sense they would want any harm to come to you if they're making a financial investment in your future," Sean said. "Still, I'd like to speak to them directly. It never hurts to ask a few questions. Dig around long enough and we'll find something. Even if we end up back at the beginning with a genuine fan-turned-stalker who was savvy enough to hire the company to find her."

A shiver raced down her spine at the thought another dead body could turn up. She might not know who Anton Miles was but that didn't mean his death mattered less. Had he been trying to get close enough to shoot her the other day? Because he probably could have gotten off a clean shot if that had been his intention.

"You mentioned something about a rival of Mitch's," she said, switching gears. Was it next to impossible to think anyone in her inner circle could be responsible for any of this? Yes. It was. She couldn't imagine someone wanting to hurt her.

"Drake Johnson," he confirmed. She realized he was probably going out on a limb telling her the name, since Sean's work seemed to fall under the category of *classified.*

"And why would he be a threat to me?" she asked, hoping they could get somewhere with this change in direction.

"The two are longtime rivals. Mitch has made mistakes. He'll be the first to admit it," Sean said. "If it turns out that you are Mitch's daughter, Drake would have reason to come at you in order to hurt Mitch."

"I don't have children. Never thought about becoming a mother, really. But that seems like the best way to get back at a person. I've heard children described as being a person's heart walking around outside their body," she said.

"I'm with you on never wanting kids of my own," he said. "And I agree one hundred percent that I'd go to the ends of the earth to protect mine if my situation changed."

The image of their baby in Sean's arms wasn't something Raelynn had expected to see or like. And yet, there it was all the same.

Pushing the thought aside, she had questions about why someone would hire Mitch to find his own daughter and then do what? Kill her? Did that mean she would be forced to take the DNA test to get answers once and for all?

Chapter Ten

The idea Drake could have set up a fake identity to make Mitch locate his own daughter was brilliant revenge. Mitch would never forgive himself if anything happened to his only child, especially if he led the killer to her doorstep. Was murder the endgame, though? There were other possibilities, like abduction and torture. Of course, all the scenarios led to an eventual death, but Drake could take this to a whole new level of hell for Mitch.

"The DNA test might bring answers to the investigation," he finally said after a thoughtful pause.

"How so?" Raelynn asked, nursing the cup of coffee from half an hour ago.

He explained his line of thinking.

"What did Mitch do to this Drake person that would make him want to exact revenge to this degree?" she asked, clearly shaken that someone with the kinds of skills Sean and Mitch possessed could be after her.

"It's Mitch's story to tell," Sean said, not wanting

to taint her opinion of the person who might end up being her father.

"Mitch is a good person, right?" she asked.

"He saved my life and the lives of countless others," he said. "There's no doubt in my mind that he's the best. I've never been on the wrong side of him, though. If someone intended to harm a person Mitch loved, I'd see a different side to him." This seemed like a good time to warn her about men like him in general, men like Sean. "Look. No one is all good or all bad."

"I know," she said. The look in her eyes said she had intimate experience with this idea. However, she didn't know men like Sean and Mitch. They were wired differently from others, as evidenced by the fact they both had the ability to snap someone's neck if the situation called for it. Taking a life intentionally was never easy, and they were on the side of good when it was required. And yet, killing someone took a toll even when it was righteous.

Raelynn studied him like she was trying to decipher an intricate puzzle. "Does the reason you needed saving have something to do with the tremors in your hands sometimes?"

There was no reason to lie, considering he'd already told her about the kid. Thinking about the way he'd lost his best friends caused guilt to take hold.

"Yes," he said. "I came back a mess. Mitch heard about me and asked if I wanted to come here to work in the office. Do paperwork."

"What did you say?" she asked.

"That I wasn't an accountant and didn't need anyone's pity," he quipped. "I was full of myself and angry at the world after what happened."

"And now?"

"I'm just angry," he said in a rare moment of complete honesty. "You'd think it would have gone away by now. I've learned to live with it. Doc said I should give it a name."

"Did you?" she asked.

"Stanley," he confessed. "You'd think I would have given it some tough name like Tyson or Rocky. But, no, Stanley came to mind, so I kept it."

"Hearing the name Tyson makes me want to fight someone," she said. "Stanley, on the other hand, doesn't seem so bad. Stanley might be your neighbor or a guy who helps you when you need to fix your plumbing but have no idea how and there are no good tutorials on YouTube."

"Maybe that's what I was thinking underneath all the layers," he said, figuring she wasn't too far off base. It would be difficult to stay angry at someone named Stanley. It was a peaceful name. Stanley was smart and possibly wore glasses. He was an accountant, the guy who took care of people's taxes or helped them pull their vehicle out of a ditch. Stanley wasn't someone who put on boxing gloves and then stayed in the ring until one of them couldn't walk out again.

Sean chuckled. His reaction seemed to cause Raelynn to laugh. Her voice was already musical. Her laugh would diffuse the worst of situations. No one could stay frustrated around a sound like the beauty of her laughter. He wasn't immune.

"Stanley did his job," she said. "He made you laugh."

"You did that," he quickly countered, realizing there was something special about Raelynn—so much so that when she walked out of his life, there would be a permanent scar in the place she currently occupied in his heart.

Where did that come from?

Sean wasn't exactly one to wax poetic. He wasn't the type of person who needed anyone else. He'd done fine on his own. The irony in his statement bit back. He'd done mostly fine on his own. Mitch had stepped in when Sean didn't believe he could keep going. His buddy Fox had linked the two five years ago.

"How long have you worked with Mitch?" Raelynn asked. It dawned on Sean that she was digging around for information on the person who might be her father, even though she claimed she didn't want to know the truth.

"Five years now," he said. "Mitch is a good man. I'm not accusing him of being perfect, but perfection is an unattainable goal anyway."

She nodded on that statement so enthusiastically it was obvious she agreed.

"I'm not sure where my life would be right now if it wasn't for Mitch and a guy by the name of Fox," Sean admitted.

Raelynn rolled the coffee mug around in her palms. "Who is he and how did you meet?"

"Fox has a place in East Texas where the military sends guys like me to cool off before reentry into civilized society," he said.

"Meaning?"

"Until we're not deemed a threat," he said. "Coming off live action, we're pretty wired, so we need some time to reacclimate to normal life. Fox's ranch is where some of us are sent. I ended up there roughly five years ago, but I was a complete mess."

She kept studying him without speaking and there was no judgment in her eyes, just compassion.

"To say that I was broken is an understatement," he continued. "You think my hands are bad now. You should have seen them back then." He held them up and forced them to shake almost uncontrollably. "This is what they used to look like." He picked up his coffee mug and then took a sip. "Now? They have episodes, but it's manageable."

"I'm sorry that happened to you, Sean," she said. The compassion in her voice made him want to reach out to her in order to have some physical contact, some reminder that he was still human.

"Worse things have—"

"Don't do that to yourself," she said. "The pain you've been through is enormous. You don't have to minimize it. All I can say is how much I admire you for still standing after everything you've been through."

"I could say the same thing about you," he stated,

turning the tables. "You survived an orphanage as a kid. That couldn't have been easy. Plus, you were too young to defend yourself. You weren't trained in combat like I was."

"No, I wasn't," she agreed. "Those were some of the hardest years of my life. But the great thing about childhood is that it's short. Those experiences made me strong. Not needing anyone else is a superpower."

Was it, though? Sean had sold himself a similar line most of his life. But then he'd never been around anyone like Raelynn before. She made him want to need someone more than he needed to breathe.

"IF YOU'RE ASKING me about Mitch, I can confirm one hundred percent that he's a more decent person than most anyone I've ever known," Sean said. There was a quality in his tone that she couldn't quite pinpoint. Defensiveness?

"Do you know why he believes I'm his daughter?" she asked, figuring she might as well go all in at this point. Even if he knew, he might not feel at liberty to tell her.

"No idea," he said with the kind of certainty that said he was being totally honest. "Believe it or not, we don't sit around and share a lot of personal details with each other. We go out back and shoot hoops. We work side by side when necessary. We're a team in every sense of the word. I know when he's going to go left while on the ground with one look or by the tone of his voice. But we've never gone out for a beer or had a casual conversation about each other's family lives."

"How do you know whether or not he has a wife or other kids?" she asked. She could identify with every word. The loneliest feeling in the world came when she was surrounded by a crowd but felt completely by herself. Sean's statement also made her realize he could have a personal life she knew nothing about. Was there someone in the background? Someone he already knew? Someone who could be special?

Raelynn was mortified by her actions now. The kiss should never have happened.

"I don't," he said. "Not with one-hundred-percent certainty."

"Why not?" she continued, curious about how his world worked.

"Easy." He said like it was plain as the nose on her face. "Information about someone is power in our world. Take you, for example. If Drake found out about you, he'd be able to use that information against Mitch."

"By kidnapping, torturing or murdering me," she said, low and under her breath.

"Think what that would be like if you had a kid or a spouse," he continued. "Which is why it's best for us not to have any of those things as long as we work here."

"I'm guessing that goes double for Mitch," she said. A thought struck. "Would it be better if we never figured out if I was his daughter, then? I mean, what about me disappearing and never coming back?

Couldn't you set me up with a new identity? We'd kill two birds with one stone by tricking my stalker in the process."

"Is that what you want? To disappear?" he asked. "You'd have to give up songwriting altogether. Your new job would have to be in a completely different industry. You'd have to walk away from everything you've created."

"Seems like I'm a liability here," she said before putting her hand up, palm out. "I'm not looking for sympathy in that statement. I'm being practical. If I'm Mitch's daughter, that opens up a whole can of worms. Right?"

"That's one way to look at it," he said after a thoughtful pause. "You could also say figuring this out is a good thing. It might not be Drake pulling the strings and you wouldn't have to go public with your father/daughter relationship if that was the case. The information could stay buried. If the DNA test comes up with a match, you would have extra security for the rest of your life. There's no way Mitch would let anyone intent to do you harm get within five feet of you."

She nodded, trying to assess the risks and the possible benefits. This world was outside her realm of understanding. Hiding people. Finding people. Making people disappear. It sounded like a cloak-and-dagger world.

"Here's the thing, though. I don't want anything from him," she reiterated for clarification purposes. The guy must make a decent amount of money from an operation like this. Wouldn't he expect his heir to go after it?

"He wouldn't force a relationship," Sean defended. "He isn't built that way. Plus, we had a discussion about the paternity test the other day. He won't ask you to take it again. It's completely up to you."

"Being this close to a possible answer must be driving him mad," she said. "He strikes me as the kind of person who gets things done, not someone who goes with the flow."

"Those two things don't have to compete against each other," Sean said.

"Okay, but he should protect his company. The man has no idea who I am or what I'm capable of," she said. "I could go after him financially, make his life difficult or both. I could be a hot mess. Why wouldn't he be at least a little bit concerned about my mental state?"

"He wouldn't care," Sean said, then held up his index finger. "That's not exactly true. He would care a whole helluva lot. The difference between Mitch and most everyone else is that he wouldn't give up."

"Even if I turned out to be a liability to him?" she asked, wondering if she'd inherited any of this—*if* he turned out to be her father. Right now, that was a big if. She probably shouldn't be overly fixated on the fact Mitch had hazel eyes and a reddish tint to otherwise dark hair. Or the fact their noses looked surprisingly similar, even though hers was a much smaller version.

"The people he takes on come out of the military

in so many broken pieces that half the time we've given up on ourselves long before we arrive here," Sean stated. There was nothing but admiration in his voice when he spoke about Mitch. She'd noticed it early on and Sean was consistent on that point. "We've been damaged in some way physically."

He held up hands that had a slight tremor as though she needed a visual reminder.

"But that's just the scars people can see," he continued. "The real work is in here." He pointed toward his skull. "We're trained killers who have been disillusioned by a job we went into willingly. Let a few of those words sink in for a minute. We are *trained* to *kill*. We are broken. We are at the worst of rock bottom because we're also coming back into the country hot, which means tempers aren't exactly back under control. The government likes to keep this a secret, but we're a threat to civilians if someone looks at us the wrong way."

"You're not like that, Sean," she said quietly as she stared into eyes filled with anguish and guilt.

"I'm no different than any of those others," he argued. "The point is that Mitch never gave up on us. Not one of us. He had no reason to help us or offer us sanctuary, let alone a job. There was no reason that man should have cared about our futures. But he did. And that's how I know he wouldn't give up on his kid, even if that kid was a train wreck."

"A person like that deserves a break, too," she said, figuring there was no amount of arguing in the world that would convince Sean he was special.

At least, he was to her. The feeling was taking root, growing, making her wish for things she probably shouldn't, despite knowing they were exactly what she wanted.

Chapter Eleven

An overwhelming sense of guilt reared its ugly head, trying to suck Sean under and churn him out once again. He took three slow, deep breaths. It was strange how remembering to breathe helped in times like these. Taking air in and out of his lungs wasn't something he normally had to think about.

Without realizing, his hands had fisted. Flexing and releasing his fingers gave some relief from the tension building. Even with the tools he had available to him, thinking about the past was never easy. Talking about it with Raelynn and seeing the compassion in her eyes meant a whole lot to him.

"Only you can decide what you're willing to do or not do, but you're not wrong about Mitch. He's one of the good ones and deserves a break. He'd never turn his back on any one of us," Sean pointed out.

"I can think of another person who deserves a break," she said softly, before adding, "You."

Before he could respond, the sound of someone entering the compound broke through. It was the phase one alert signal and he figured it was about time for Mitch to return. Sean fished his cell phone out of his pocket and checked the screen, confirming his suspicion.

"It's Mitch," he stated.

Raelynn quietly refilled her coffee cup as the second alert triggered. Not thirty seconds later, the hum of Mitch's truck could be heard out front. The engine cut off and he walked through the front door with a weary look.

"Everything all right?" Sean asked before walking over and greeting Mitch with a bear hug. The conversation with Raelynn reminded Sean how lucky he'd been that Mitch had welcomed him into the fold.

"The tech worker," Mitch said before he acknowledged Raelynn and then walked over to the fridge to empty the couple of bags he held with his left hand. "Anton Miles. Turns out, he had a pregnant wife. The guy has only been married a year and his wife is six months pregnant."

Raelynn gasped as she brought her hand up to cover her mouth. News like this would hit everyone hard.

"Does that mean he's a scapegoat?" Sean asked.

"It looks that way," Mitch confirmed.

"Raises suspicion against Drake since he has reason to get back at you, doesn't it?" Sean continued.

"He is supposedly out of the country right now, according to his assistant," Mitch said before issuing a sharp sigh.

"You don't believe it," Sean confirmed.

"Not a chance," Mitch said as he moved to the

cabinet for a mug. He turned toward Raelynn. "Did you eat?"

"Yes," she said. "I had plenty. Thank you." She seemed genuinely touched by the gesture. That was Mitch. He looked after people when he came into contact with them, plain and simple. No blood connection needed. Mitch had a heart bigger than his chest. Anyone could count themselves lucky for Mitch to be their father.

Mitch poured a cup of coffee. The room stayed quiet as he turned around and then set the mug down on the granite island. Stress cracks showed on his forehead and it looked like he wasn't getting any sleep.

"When's the last time you ate?" Sean asked his boss.

Mitch glanced up at the ceiling like he was trying to recall the information. "A while ago."

"How about a sandwich to go with that coffee?" Sean asked but he was already making his way toward the fridge.

"I can do it myself," Mitch argued but Sean waved him off.

Out of the corner of his eye, he watched Raelynn walk over to the desk where the DNA kit sat. She picked up the box as Sean pulled out all the necessary ingredients. He didn't make a show of watching what happened next. Raelynn set the box down in front of him.

"What do you need from me?" she asked.

The move, the offer, the change in topic seemed

to catch Mitch off guard. It took him a few seconds to recover. He cleared his throat. "This one works with a hair sample or saliva, I believe."

Raelynn picked up the box again. She read the back of it as Sean finished assembling the sandwich. He placed the snack on a plate.

"Here you go," Sean said to Mitch as he set the offering down in front of his boss. "Might help make the coffee go down better."

Mitch shoved the coffee a little farther away from the plate. "I might have been a little overly ambitious in pouring it. I'll grab water instead."

"I got it," Sean said. "Go ahead and eat." He retrieved a glass from the cabinet next to the sink and filled it before bringing it over and setting it down next to the plate.

Despite the heavy circumstances, Mitch smirked.

"What's that all about?" Sean asked.

"You're turning into me," Mitch said before taking a bite.

Sean opened his mouth to argue but no words came out. The statement wasn't all that far from the truth, so Sean threw his hands in the air, palms up in the surrender position. "Look at that. Turns out, I'm trainable after all."

"I always knew you could do whatever you set your mind to," Mitch said with a proud-papa smile. Chest out, he practically beamed. Well, maybe *beamed* was pushing it. The man did, however, look like he'd just watched his kid take his first steps.

Sean's mind was beginning to create an argument

for opening his heart a little to the woman standing two feet away from him. Could he?

RAELYNN HAD FACED more challenges in her almost thirty-one years on this earth than most did in a lifetime. Taking a DNA test shouldn't make her want to run out the front door and keep going until she dropped from exhaustion or crossed a state line, whichever came first.

The thought made her realize how tired she was from being on the run. The idea of staying in hiding or this situation dragging on much longer made her chest tighten. Besides, where would she go?

Sticking around in a relationship wasn't her best trait. Being on the road ensured she didn't have to take any chances. When she wasn't on the road, she was holed up, writing songs and making new music. If she wasn't careful, the cycle of travel-songwriting-travel could become a grind and she would lose all the love she had for her work.

Steadying her hands, she continued to read the side of the DNA box. A hair sample would do. With a deep breath, she decided to go for it.

"I'll go grab my brush," she said before setting the box down again. Walking out of the room was easier than she thought it would be. Putting one foot in front of the other seemed so basic, but she'd learned to break down impossible seeming tasks by doing just that. She could make it to the bottom of the stairs. She could climb them one by one. She could make it to the bathroom where her hairbrush sat on the countertop. Thankfully, she'd kept a small one inside her crossbody bag that was always secured over her shoulder in case all hell broke loose. She'd learned early on to keep her ID, credit cards and cash with her at all times, even when she slept. There was a small travel kit inside the bag that allowed her to brush her teeth at pretty much any kind of water source. She'd slipped into a diner's bathroom. She'd used a bottle of water in the woods. The tent was a real loss. Although didn't Sean say he'd wrapped her guitar case in the tent to keep it from getting soaked and ruined?

She glanced at the bed as she passed by. Last night had been a shock. No wonder her body had been stiff when she'd woken up, considering she'd been asleep for almost a full day. So much had happened in the past day and a half she needed a minute to process the events. The thought of a wife losing her new husband and a baby losing its father before entering the world carved a hole in her chest.

Did she know anyone who wanted to get back at her enough to kill another human being? Or was Anton Miles guilty? What was his involvement and could he be tied back to Drake? And were either of them connected to her stalker?

Since none of those questions could be answered right now, she shelved them before heading downstairs.

"Here you go," she said to Mitch, handing over the hairbrush with plenty of strands. "I don't want to know the results, but I think you deserve to."

Mitch's forehead creased like he didn't understand her logic.

"I just want you to be able to get closure," she said. "You seem like a really good person. Sean here has been telling me about how you saved his life."

Mitch opened his mouth to protest.

"It's true," Sean stated, cutting his boss off before the man could form an argument.

"You do know it's impossible for me to save anyone's life," Mitch eventually got out. "All I do is assist someone who is ready to help themselves. None of this is possible if you aren't willing to put in the work. I just help with the tools."

"Since there isn't exactly a line of people doing the same, it would probably be a good idea to recognize what you do for people before they can do it for themselves," Sean pointed out. "I wasn't ready to acknowledge any of my issues and now I can see the light of day because of you."

"Fair enough," Mitch conceded.

"You're the miracle man," Sean said.

"Too bad not everyone shares your opinion," Mitch stated, clearly referring back to Drake. "I've never claimed to be perfect."

Raelynn watched as the scene unfolded. She saw the dynamic happening between Sean and Mitch. Their connection brought out a longing in her that she'd tucked away so deep she didn't realize it was there any longer. The desire to belong to a family wasn't something she'd allowed herself to think about, let alone want. How strange was that? Not since she was a little girl had she dreamed of big family dinners at Christmas. The image was still clear in her mind, though. There would be more presents than anyone could count, even though she didn't care so much about material possessions. It would be about being together and making memories. It would be about cookies with too much brown sugar and eggnog that was spiked with spiced rum. It would be about sitting around a massive table as conversation and laughter filled the room. The whole scenario would be wrapped up in a red bow, complete with hot chocolate next to a crackling fire. She'd gone all in with the Norman Rockwell image of what the holidays should be. Growing up in an orphanage without presents or a whole lot of cheer had given her a lot of time to fantasize. Becoming an adult had meant discarding childish ideas. Besides, those hopes had died a long time ago. So why were they resurfacing now?

Witnessing the father/son bond between Sean and Mitch nearly brought tears to her eyes. There was a whole lot of love and respect between those two men. From what she could see here, family didn't have to come only from those who shared DNA. Sometimes, if someone was really lucky, family chose.

Speaking of which, hadn't Sean said he came from a big family? She'd recognized the last name but wasn't familiar with the details. Raelynn couldn't help but wonder what his siblings were like. What about his mother? Father? Did he have grandparents who were still alive?

Those were the questions trying to penetrate her

skull. She wanted to know more about Sean and his personal life. But he'd been clear. His personal life was off-limits when it came to his work. So, why was that so difficult to accept?

"I'll keep the test results to myself," Mitch assured. "But I can't promise that you won't be able to figure it out for yourself. Either way, I'll commit to leaving you alone. It's clear that you don't want someone showing up in your life after all these years whether I'm your biological parent or not."

"Would you mind telling me why you think that you're my father in the first place?" she asked, wondering if she should have gone down that road when his expression shifted.

"Are you sure you want to know?" he asked.

"Yes," she said, wondering why he would ask the question. Was there some dark secret that might hurt her?

Mitch retrieved his cell phone. He used his thumbprint to get past its security. The screen lit up a moment later. It didn't take long for him to flip through photos to land on the one he seemed to be looking for.

"This is her," he said as he tilted the screen for Raelynn to get a better view.

No, she wasn't ready for the face staring up at her. Because the resemblance was too close.

"I'm guessing she would be my mother if the test comes back positive," Raelynn said, unable and unwilling to take her gaze off the photo. The red hair

and hazel eyes, the heart-shaped face… It would be like looking into a mirror, except for the nose.

Looking at Sean right now wouldn't be the wisest move, not while she was feeling so vulnerable.

"Someone made sure that I was bombarded with news stories about your career," Mitch said. "This person must have decent tech skills, because I didn't pick up on the fact it was happening. Every time I opened a news browser, there would be a story about you. You looked so much like her…" He stopped long enough to clear his throat before continuing. "I figured you had to be her daughter. The resemblance is too close. Since your age is printed with every story, it dawned on me to do the math."

"Having a job where we get paid to pay attention to details can be a liability sometimes," Sean said when Mitch paused.

Mitch nodded, and a moment passed between them. This kind of work drew a certain type of person. These two were clearly two peas in a pod.

"Once I did the math, the possibility I could be your father smacked me in the face," Mitch stated. "It took a few days for it to sink in, even though I saw some of me in you, too. I never would have thought Annalise disappeared to have a baby."

"My nose," she said quietly. A lot of information coming at her before she had a chance to process any of it wasn't her strong suit.

And yet, the news Mitch might be her father settled over her like a warm blanket on a cold night this time around—until deep-seated panic set in.

"Where is she now?" Raelynn asked. "Why not just go to her and ask what happened?"

Mitch just shook his head. Raelynn tried to let the news sink in. Based on Mitch's reaction, it seemed that even if she wanted to, she'd never have the chance to get to know her mother.

Chapter Twelve

"Do what you want with the brush," Raelynn said before taking a couple of steps backward. Another two and her backside clashed with the lower cabinets near the sink.

The change in Raelynn had been drastic and almost instant. Sean could pinpoint the moment the air shifted. He just couldn't figure out why.

Mitch seemed taken aback by the change in her demeanor. Wide eyes that signaled fear bounced back and forth between him and Mitch, and then the exit. She needed an escape route. From what?

"Would you care to go for a walk?" he asked her.

She nodded as the tension in her face scored her forehead with stress lines. Good. If he got her outside, maybe he could get her talking. It had helped him to be able to lean on her when he was getting inside his head. Maybe the same would work for her. Or maybe he just wanted to protect her in any way he could. She deserved to have someone look out for her for a change. Her statement about never having to depend on anyone else resonated a little too well.

Hearing the words spoken out loud made him realize how lonely it could be, too.

Maybe it was time to let someone in for a change.

Raelynn darted toward the door so fast he feared she might grab the truck keys and bolt off the property while she was at it. Had seeing the picture of her possible mother struck a raw nerve? Because for a few seconds, Raelynn had seemed calm and peaceful after being shown the photo, and then all hell seemed to break loose in her mind.

"I'll make sure she's okay," Sean said quietly to a concerned Mitch.

"Thank you," Mitch whispered, biting back a yawn.

"This might be a good time for you to rest," Sean pointed out before heading to the back door.

Outside, Raelynn was pacing the length of the building. She twisted her fingers together in hyperdrive. Since the most annoying thing he could say right now was "Calm down," he stood in a wide athletic stance instead and folded his arms over his chest. All he could do at this point was hope having another person out here helped her see that she wasn't alone.

There was silence between them for a solid five minutes. It didn't matter. He could stand here all evening if she needed him to. In fact, this time of year, the sun was already starting its descent. He had to love December for its short days and long nights. There was an ironic thought. Just as calving season was about to heat up, the days became the shortest.

In fact, the shortest month was also one of the busiest on a cattle ranch.

Unsure how he'd gone from being here for Raelynn to his family's cattle ranch in Cider Creek, Sean figured his mind was spinning out because they weren't getting anywhere with the investigation.

"I look like her," Raelynn finally said, stopping ten feet away from him. She faced Sean as though they had on boxing gloves and were about to go a few rounds.

"Yes," he admitted. "But that doesn't guarantee anything."

"You can't deny the resemblance is uncanny," she continued, her chest rising and falling as though she'd run half a marathon.

"No, and I won't try," he said, dropping his hands to his sides. "If I've learned anything in life, it's that looks can be deceiving. So, I try not to judge a situation until I have facts to back up my assumptions."

"Sounds like you're telling me not to freak out until I know for certain," she said, but her tone was adversarial.

"I wouldn't dare tell you what to think or feel," he said. "You're a grown woman and have earned the right to handle yourself any way you see fit."

"Then, what? Stay calm while my future hangs in the balance?" she continued, clearly on a hot path.

"Nothing changes unless you decide to allow it," he said.

"Easy for you to say," she quipped with all the anger and fire of a teapot about to explode.

"You're right," he admitted, using as calm a voice as he could. "I have no idea what this is like for you. All I know is that I want to help however I can. The last thing I want to do is say something to make you feel worse. So, you're going to have to spell it out for me. What can I do or say to help you?"

Raelynn's stare felt more like a challenge.

"Are you in a relationship right now?" she finally asked.

"No," he said after a look of surprise at the sudden change of topic.

"There's no one special in your life out there somewhere? Waiting for you to come home?" she continued, almost daring him to tell her there was. He sure as hell didn't know where this was going.

"No one," he said. Then came, "You?"

She shook her head.

"Do you really want to know what I want from you right now?" she asked.

He nodded.

"For you to kiss me," she stated, with the kind of certainty that stirred up senses that had no business overtaking rational thought.

Rather than stand there and debate whether this was the right time to make a move, he stopped overthinking and just acted. He ate up the space between them in a few quick strides. She brought her hands up to his chest, digging her fingernails in like she was trying to anchor herself against a raging storm. Her eyes sparked with anticipation and something that looked a whole lot like desire as he brought his mouth down on hers with an intense need.

THE SECOND SEAN'S lips touched Raelynn's, trouble brewed deep inside her chest. She ignored the idea that this man could shatter her heart into a thousand flecks of dust. This was exactly what she wanted—and needed—from him.

Raelynn parted her lips and teased his tongue inside her mouth, which didn't take a whole lot of effort. Her breath quickened, matching the tempo of his pulse—a pulse she could feel underneath her fingertips as they pressed deeper against the muscles of his chest. Touching Sean was supposed to anchor her. Instead, electrical impulses vibrated through her.

There was more passion and heat in this kiss than in any she'd ever experienced. She'd known on instinct Sean was special, and this moment happening between them proved she could still trust her intuition.

Rather than pull back, he seemed to lean into the kiss as he looped his arms around her waist and tugged her closer until their bodies were flush. Sparks practically flew at every point of contact, and she could only imagine what skin to bare naked skin would feel like with this man. The image of their bodies in a tangle, arms and legs entwined, sent warmth rocketing through her, circling low in her belly.

This time she was the one who slowed down the momentum. Eyes still closed, he pressed his forehead to hers. She could breathe in his breath. The dark roast coffee tasted so much better on Sean's lips.

A few deep breaths only managed to bring in more of his spicy scent. Raelynn forced herself to shift her attention to something that didn't cause her pulse to skyrocket. The kisses had worked their magic anyway. She'd been fully distracted and immersed in everything that was Sean.

It wouldn't last...*couldn't* last. She needed to get her mind back into reality, and the very real possibility a highly trained assassin might want her dead. At the very least, he wanted to use her to torture Mitch. But that wasn't the only reason.

For another long moment, she stood there as the sun disappeared. The only sounds besides their breathing came from crickets chirping. Even those noises were drowned out by the sound of her own heartbeat.

"Should we go inside?" she finally asked Sean.

"Whenever you're ready," he said, his low timbre washing over her and through her, causing butterflies to release inside her. The sensation of cliff diving nearly took her breath away. "Or we could stay out here. Talk about whatever it is that's running through your mind."

He reached for her hand and then linked their fingers before walking over to a wooden swing facing the expansive backyard. It had occurred to her when they'd first driven in that having a big open space back there made it difficult for anyone to sneak up on the house. There wasn't much to hide behind. It was smart to keep the area clear. The other safeguards reminded her just how dire her own situation was that she would need to be here at all.

She sat down on the swing, and Sean leaned against the railing holding it up.

“I’m not good at talking,” she said to him, wishing she could get some of this off her chest.

“That’s okay. I’m a patient man,” he reassured. “Plus, we don’t have to start with anything big. How about telling me your favorite color?”

“Easy,” she said with a small smile. “That’s blue like the sky on an early summer day.”

“Blue’s a good color,” he agreed. “And there isn’t much better than that time of year, until fall.”

“Crisp mornings, right?” she said, without hesitation or worry about how the words might come out.

“Orange is my second favorite,” she continued after agreeing. “But not like a pumpkin. More like the color of leaves as they fall to the ground.”

“Looks like we have a couple of things in common,” he said with a smile that threatened to blow past all her defenses.

She exhaled, *really* exhaled, in a way she hadn’t done in far too long.

“You’re wondering what freaked me out a little while ago,” she said, motioning toward the seat next to her on the bench swing.

He nodded as he moved toward her, sitting so close the outsides of their thighs touched. More of that warmth flooded her, leaving a trail of sensual vibrations in its wake.

"I'm here if you want to talk," he said in a voice that made her want to open up and spill all her secrets. "Even if you just need to say words until something makes sense."

"It's her," she said. "Mitch showed me the picture and I felt something. It's hard to describe except to say there was a connection I've never experienced before."

"Why isn't that a good thing?" he asked. There was something about his presence, about him sitting next to her, touching, that calmed her.

"I looked at her and saw me," she tried to explain.

"Which was good for a minute, but then not so much," he continued, as though teasing the words out of her. It helped.

"Right," she said on a sigh. "I'd gotten to the point, long ago, where I didn't miss having parents."

"Now, you don't want to go back to that place where you once did miss it," he said as her fears seemed to dawn on him. He was perceptive, and good at figuring her out. Then again, that was his job.

"Not willingly, no," she admitted. "The disappointment hurts too much. Plus, I made a promise to myself a long time ago that I would never feel that kind of pain again."

He sat there for a long moment before speaking.

"I'm the last one who should be talking about this, considering everything you're saying has been a mantra for me at one time or another in my life," he finally said. "But how do you ever let anyone in if you're always afraid of getting hurt?"

"I don't," she said. Those two words, spoken out loud in this context, made her see how lonely that must sound. "I have my work and I date around. It's not like I spend every moment of my life alone." She could also hear the defensiveness in her own voice and realized he'd struck a nerve.

Sean's hand enclosed hers.

"I'm just as bad," he said. "With me, work is always a good excuse to keep people at arm's length. Being messed up makes it easy to push people away—to convince yourself that you're doing it for them, when in reality it's not true."

Those words resonated more than she wanted them to.

"Turns out, we're not so different," she said to him.

"Can I ask what would happen *if* Mitch is your father and the woman in the photograph was your mother?" he continued.

"I haven't gotten that far," she said. "I mean, I'm grown so the parenting ship has sailed. I guess I understand why my mother would have kept me from him considering how young they would have been. Neither would have been able to figure out what to do with me."

"I don't know anything about your mother, if that's what we're looking at here," Sean started. "But I can vouch for Mitch. It wouldn't matter how young he was. He would have done the right thing by you."

"I'm getting that sense," she said, realizing just how much of a great person Mitch seemed to be. What about her mother?

"Your mother probably had her reasons for keeping you from him," he continued. "She probably thought it would be in his best interests not to know about you."

"I guess so," she said, although she couldn't imagine a scenario where that would turn out well.

"Until we know the circumstances, it might be best to not make assumptions or judgments," he defended. "Believe me when I say that I've seen a whole lot in this job—more than most. But then, that covers my whole life, too."

"I want to think the best of this situation," she admitted. "I do." She paused a moment to collect her thoughts. "But what if that's not the case here? No one can guarantee she was a good person or had good intentions."

"That's true," he said after a thoughtful pause. "The only thing I can say is that I know Mitch and he doesn't strike me as the type who would get involved with someone lightly. I have to think your mother had a good reason for what she did—*if* they turn out to be your parents."

"I guess the hair sample will tell us for sure," she said, thinking she wasn't quite ready to give the woman a break. Could she handle knowing the truth?

Chapter Thirteen

All Sean could do at this point was hold Raelynn. There was no amount of talking that could make any of this easier on her. So, he didn't try. Instead, he reached his arm around her shoulders and held her. She leaned into him and all kinds of fireworks exploded in his chest. Whatever was happening between them was beyond any level of attraction he'd experienced to date.

Was he ready for something of this magnitude?

A killer seemed determined to cut his relationship with Raelynn short. Sitting there on the swing, he realized he wasn't going home to the ranch anytime soon. He reached for his cell phone with his free hand.

Raelynn was already resting her head on his shoulder, and it was the most amazing thing he'd felt in far too long. There was something very right about this moment. She'd opened up to him and given him a peek inside her thoughts. Letting his emotions run wild probably wasn't his smartest idea. And yet, being around Raelynn made him want things he probably shouldn't. She had an incredible ability to make him believe somehow everything would work out in life. It was rare, and he considered it her superpower. Or maybe it was just the hold she had on him. A growing piece of him wanted to be able to give her the world. Security was a given. Not only was it his job to make sure she stayed alive, but he wanted to be her protector, which was foreign to him. Because of his past, he didn't do protection details. This would normally be a good time for him to bow out of a mission—except that everything inside him wanted to stick around and make sure Raelynn stayed safe. The thought Drake could be behind this was an unsettling idea at best.

The last thing he wanted was for her to feel trapped in Texas. This was her home, and she deserved to be able to stay here and continue all the amazing work she was already doing.

"Hey." Raelynn's voice broke through his heavy thoughts. She was like the sun finally breaking through clouds on a stormy day.

"Sorry," he said, apologizing for zoning out and getting lost in his own thoughts.

"You don't ever need to apologize to me, Sean," she stated. "I wondered where you went just now."

"Mitch being your father or not isn't really the biggest problem we're facing right now," he reminded her. "There's someone out there whose identity needs to be revealed, and he has to be stopped before this gets out of hand." His chest hurt at the thought that anything might happen to Raelynn. Not on his watch. And he hoped like hell he could keep that promise.

"I know," she said quietly. "But we'll get this figured out if it's the last thing we do."

He didn't want to point out that was exactly what was at stake here—her life. And he would never be able to face the mirror again if he allowed anything to happen to her.

"Mitch is following up on Drake's possible involvement," Sean said, thinking out loud.

"Yes," she agreed. "He seems like a strong possibility considering he would have resources to handle the technology that might be involved in locating her through Sean, and he would be intelligent enough to set something like this up."

"Don't forget vengeful enough to want to pull this off," Sean warned. The thought of someone like Drake setting his sights on Raelynn was a gut punch. Sean didn't like to think Mitch had an equivalent out there, someone darker who was willing to break rules to get what he wanted. Then again, Razor-Sharp existed for a reason. The organization came about to right wrongs and help folks disappear from men like Drake.

"Right. That."

Raelynn shivered, so he tightened his arm around her even though he suspected she wasn't cold.

"Since Mitch is working that angle, we can focus on the stalker," he said.

"You don't think it was this Anton person, do you?" she asked.

"Not for the time being," he clarified. "Later on, we can see if there's any connection but I'd like to treat them as separate entities for now."

"Okay," she said.

"Tell me more about the situation with the stalker," he said. "Give me a sense of how it all started and what steps were taken to prevent him from getting to you."

Raelynn's sigh was like a thick, heavy rain cloud overhead before the first droplets fell.

"In the beginning, I always felt a presence lingering around after a show," she said. "There would be a figure in the distance just far enough away that I couldn't make the person out clearly. A lone incident here and there wouldn't have been a blip on my radar. I do have a handful of fans who travel from show to show when I'm on tour."

"This was different, though," he said.

"My diehards usually sign up for meet and greets. They make it very obvious they're there to see me and give me a hug or shake my hand. This was more like a secret admirer feeling," she said.

"It must have escalated," he said.

"It did," she admitted. "A single flower would show up tucked in the windshield of my tour bus. I got a message earlier that said, 'get back on stage or die' and then my stalker stole personal garments of mine from backstage. Sadly, not entirely unexpected in my career. As artists, we're encouraged to engage with fans to get them excited about our work. To be honest, it was the most difficult part of the job for me." She sucked in a breath. "But keep in mind a really great day in my book is being in a cool dark room alone with my guitar while the words flow."

He could relate to the being alone part. It had never felt lonely until recently, though. He chalked it up to being restless in general. As much as he cared about Razor-Sharp, he was getting the itch to make a change and move on.

"It's hard to imagine you getting up on stage night after night now that I know this about you," he said honestly. "It must be torture."

"That's a good word for it," she said with a laugh that was like a cool breeze on a hot day. "Once I get going, I'm a lot better. The part I like is seeing how the crowd reacts to my songs and the music."

"I heard you strumming on the guitar," he said. "You're good."

"Thank you," she said as a blush crawled up her neck. Embarrassment shouldn't be sexy on a person, except pretty much everything would be on her. "It means a lot to hear that coming from you."

"You're welcome," he said, reaching for her hand. He gave a squeeze meant to offer reassurance, but it sent his own pulse climbing instead. Physical contact with Raelynn wasn't his smartest move considering he should probably pull back. It wasn't happening and wasn't likely to, but it was worth considering an effort to stay objective on this mission. Speaking of which, he said, "About this mystery person who hit your radar. You were right to go with your gut instincts. Too many times, people ignore them and life goes south real quick."

"You don't grow up the way I did and not have a well-developed danger radar," she admitted. The thought of her suffering caused a tightness in his chest that made it hard to breathe.

"No, I guess you don't."

"It's gotten me this far," she reassured him, as though she'd picked up on his anger at a child having to fend for themselves. As much as he'd grown to despise his grandfather over the years, Sean had never gone to bed hungry unless it was his own fault and he was too tired to walk back downstairs. There had never been a lack of food in the house. Despite Duncan Hayes driving a wedge between himself and Sean, there had been no doubt he would always have a roof over his head if he needed one. Those basics had been so easy to take for granted, and now, Sean felt like a fool for allowing his grandfather to make him feel like he hadn't belonged at the ranch or in Cider Creek, the town he loved.

"You shouldn't have needed it," he said under his breath. "No one should, especially not a defenseless child."

"Agreed," she said. "Which is also why I never plan on having one. If anything happened to me, the child could end up in the same situation."

"No child of mine would," he interjected, and then it was his turn to be embarrassed. He'd jumped the gun there. For the first time, though, he didn't hate the idea of becoming a father. If he had someone like Raelynn as a partner, he could see himself being happy.

"I believe it," Raelynn said before he could backtrack and explain that he wasn't talking about having a child with her. The reassurance hit him square in the chest, flooding him with warmth.

Sean was in trouble when it came to the beauty sitting next to him. He just wasn't exactly sure how far it went and how difficult it was going to be to recover from once she was gone.

RAELYNN LEANED INTO SEAN, something she rarely ever did with anyone. In fact, she couldn't recall one time in her life that she'd wanted to pull from someone else's strength. She'd always looked at that as weakness. Now, she was beginning to realize how much strength it took to allow herself to depend on someone else. She had to fight every deeply-rooted instinct inside her to even admit she might need a hand. This whole experience was opening her eyes to how exhausting it could be to push everyone away.

"We should take a look at the people around you first and foremost," he said. "You mentioned a couple's names before. Who are they and what do they have to gain being connected to you?"

"Let's see," she started, appreciating getting the conversation back on track. "Erik and Ashley Bradshaw have a vested interest in me. They financially support my tours and are the ones who have been able to connect me to some bigger stars on the circuit."

"Sounds like they would lose money if anything happened to you," he said.

"You wouldn't know it based on their texts," she quipped. "They kept a steady stream going telling me that it was imperative I get back on the tour and stay on it until I ditched my cell."

"Doesn't sound like someone who has your best interests at heart," he stated. "If they are backing you, can't they provide better security?"

"The cost of touring is already high enough," she said. "We get a budget to work with and I have to use most of it to pay my bandmates and my crew. Then there's insurance on top of everything else that comes out of the same budget. By the time it gets to paying me, we have to be on tour a couple of weeks before I start getting a portion of the receipts on the back end. It can take a month or two before any money starts rolling in for me. In fact, this time, Ashley said she would pick up the insurance extra. All I had to do was sign, and that saved a decent amount of money. If she bundled the policy in with some of their other investments, we could get a better price."

"Extra security sounds out of the question," he said. "But you have me now, so you shouldn't need it."

The sound of those words comforted her a great deal more than they should've. She didn't doubt Sean's abilities, but she needed to stay sharp and protect herself. After all, the best line of defense for any person was him or herself.

"It's good for me to stay vigilant," she pointed out.

The comment seemed to deflate a little bit of air out of his chest, but to his credit he didn't argue. To a trained ex-military soldier like him, he could easily take her remark as an insult.

"Everyone should," he said, feeling a little chill in his tone. Maybe he'd taken her comment a little more to heart than she realized. On an exhale, he added, "What was the tone of their texts?"

"They weren't thrilled with me for leaving the tour," she stated. "I'd show you the messages but I got rid of my phone after my stalker found me at a motel I checked in to."

"That's serious," Sean said as she sat up a little straighter.

"It was creepy," she said. "I notified the police but they said no crime had been committed yet. They offered to sign me up for crime prevention classes, which was a nice try but didn't exactly help in my case."

"Women have died in similar situations while waiting for the perp to cross a sufficient line for police," he said, shaking his head. "It's criminal the way we treat victims."

"I couldn't agree more," she admitted, missing his warm body now that she'd shifted her weight and they were sitting side by side without touching. He'd released her hand, too. This was probably for the best, so she could think more clearly. It was a little too easy to get lost in Sean Hayes.

"I'd still like to speak to Ashley and Erik, to pick their brains if nothing else," he said. "Since they have a financial interest in your return to the tour, they might be digging around on their own."

"Anything is possible," she said. "We already discussed Rudy and his gambling problem."

"I'd still like to speak to him face-to-face," he said.

"That's my list," she said.

"What about rivals? How competitive is the tour?" he asked.

"I'd say everyone pretty much leaves each other alone," she said. "It's not that easy to make something of yourself in country music. When someone does or even levels up, most of us are happy for that person."

"Have you been in competition for gigs with any one band in particular?" he asked.

"No, not really," she said. She couldn't think of anyone on the circuit who would want to run her off. "The band we open for is established."

"Any rumors of affairs going on between you and any married guys on the road?" he asked. A muscle in his jaw tensed at the question.

"I stay so far away from the gossip mill that I couldn't tell you one way or another," she admitted. It didn't seem like the answer he was hoping for, but it was true. "I keep to myself mostly and I'm in good standing with my bandmates and their significant others."

"Doesn't mean there isn't any jealousy simmering underneath the surface," he said.

"I guess you're right," she said. "I'm just wondering what anyone would have to gain by harming me. If I leave the tour, no one gets paid."

"Fair enough," he conceded. "But I wouldn't count out jealousy. It's a powerful emotion capable of making some people act out in unexpected ways."

"Rudy Cannon's wife did ask him if I was more important than her a few months ago, now that I think about it," Raelynn recalled. Funny. She wouldn't have even remembered if not for this conversation.

"Then we have to interview both of them," Sean said.

Of course she realized his statement was true, even though she didn't want to ask Rudy's wife whether or not the woman thought the two of them had been having an affair at some point. The very idea was ridiculous. Music was her focus and always would be. Could there be room for anything else?

Chapter Fourteen

"Are you ready to head back inside?" Sean asked Raelynn.

"Yes, we should probably write down a few notes about everything we've talked about so far while it's still fresh on our minds," she said, then reached for his hand.

If Mitch was still awake, he might get a shock seeing Sean and Raelynn walk inside hand in hand. Would Mitch see their connection as a good thing? Sean didn't have the words to define whatever was happening between him and Raelynn. He didn't want to put it in a box, either. He decided it would be better to deal with any backlash later. Right now, he wanted to provide as much comfort to Raelynn as he could.

The downstairs was quiet. Other operatives were in the field and the administrative assistant worked remote most of the time. Mitch must be upstairs sleeping. Raelynn let go of his hand while she moved to the fridge, walking right past the over-the-counter rapid DNA kit. The results were sitting there on the counter for her to see or ignore. The home kit wouldn't be 100 percent accurate. Mitch wouldn't take any chances there. He would send out for a lab test.

"Mind if I find something in here?" Raelynn asked, motioning toward the fridge.

"Help yourself." Sean pulled out his cell and opened a note-taking app. His phone had several layers of encryption. Hackers had a better chance of breaking into the DOD. Still, he wrote in a form of code he'd developed years ago while serving in the military that he used to this day. Sean had learned a long time ago to leave nothing to chance.

Glancing up at Raelynn, he realized she was studying him.

"What?" he asked.

Her cheeks turned hot-burner-on-the-stove red.

"Nothing," she said, brushing him off. "Except to say that your forehead gets this groove when you're concentrating that's…cute."

"Cute?" he asked, thinking *cute* was for puppies. He was a grown man. The *cute* ship had sailed a long time ago. And still, he was bemused at her comment. "I'll try to aim higher next time."

"Aim at what?" Mitch asked as he walked into the kitchen.

"No big deal," Sean said, dismissing him. Instead, he redirected Mitch's attention to the kit. "Should that be sitting out in the open?"

"My bad," Mitch said before hurrying over to collect the test. "To be fair, I haven't looked at the results, either."

"Oh," Raelynn said. "Why not?"

"We'll probably have to disperse tomorrow to run down a couple of leads, so I figured it might be a good time to check then when everyone is out of the house," he said.

"What makes you think that?" she continued.

"You were clear about not wanting to know the results and I want to respect your wishes," he said. "I'm afraid you'd see it all over my face if I don't get a little time to digest whatever the box says."

"The results from this kit might not be correct," Sean warned.

"I know," Mitch stated. "One of my errands in the morning is to run the hair samples to the lab for confirmation."

It was just like Mitch to employ multiple layers. Sean figured as much.

"Thank you for honoring my request," Raelynn said. She didn't seem ready to budge at all and the news about the woman who could be her mother having died seemed to make matters worse. Raelynn had closed up with the information. Sean might have taken his family for granted, and he couldn't begin to understand how awful Mitch and Raelynn's situation must feel. For Mitch to go all these years believing he was a single man with no children and then find out he might have a daughter who could be standing in this very room. It was a lot to take in on both sides. To their credit, though, they were handling a sticky situation with a whole lot of maturity. Southerners called that *grace*.

"Always," Mitch promised. "I can't say that you won't figure it out but I'll do my best to stay quiet either way."

"I appreciate it," she said with a little more warmth in her voice than usual when talking about possible paternity.

Mitch seemed to notice, too. In all the years Sean had known Mitch, the man rarely ever smiled. Tonight, his face almost split in two.

"How about we figure out some dinner?" Sean asked, setting his phone down on the counter to help Raelynn find food.

"I'd eat anything right now," Mitch said.

"Sit down," Sean instructed. "Between the two of us, we'll figure something out."

Raelynn broke into a small smile as he moved beside her.

"What do we have in here?" he asked.

"A lot of divorced man meals," she stated, opening the freezer.

"Hey, don't judge," he teased. "Those come in handy when you need something halfway decent and only have time to pop something in the microwave. Plus, we generally come and go at different times around here. Our sleep schedules are all over the place."

She shot him the side-eye.

"I have those in my freezer, and I take them on the road," she said. "They keep me from chewing my arm off, so no judging over here. Plus, I'm a terrible cook."

"Somehow, I highly doubt it," Sean countered. "Those eggs smelled amazing."

"You don't have to go to culinary school to throw eggs into a pan with a little olive oil," she said, rolling her eyes. "Cheese pretty much masks the rest."

"Let's see here," he said as he pulled out a divorced man meal from the freezer. "Who wants lasagna?"

"I'll take it if no one else wants it," Mitch said.

Sean looked to Raelynn, who was shaking her head. He grabbed two and then set them on the counter before moving on to the next.

"This is some kind of chicken breast with what are supposed to be grilled vegetables, and it's up for grabs," Sean said.

"Sounds like my kind of meal," Raelynn said. "I saw lettuce and tomatoes in the fridge. I can throw together a salad. Who else is in?"

Both Sean and Mitch raised their hands.

"Is there garlic salt and butter?" she asked.

"Might be," Mitch responded.

"Then I can make garlic toast out of the bread that's left," she continued.

"And here you said that you couldn't cook," Sean teased.

She elbowed him in the ribs. The gentle contact managed to set off a fireworks show of Independence Day proportions. There were two things on his mind fighting for attention: the kisses they'd shared that were burned into his memory, for one; the other was the case. His brain constantly churned over the latter even when he tried to focus on something else. Most times, in fact, it worked out better when he distracted himself. His brain had a way of chipping away at a problem in the back of his mind. Sean noticed Raelynn checked the spot where the DNA test had been more than once while she gathered ingredients. It was gone now, but that didn't stop her. Did she want to know the results more than she was willing to admit to herself?

After zapping the dinners one by one in the microwave, he emptied the contents onto plates that Raelynn had retrieved. Since agents came and went here with no one keeping an exact schedule, there wasn't a dining table. The conference table would work just fine, though.

As they all took a seat, he couldn't help but think this felt a whole lot like family.

RAELYNN EXCUSED HERSELF the second her plate was clear. She moved into the kitchen before she could get too comfortable. Despite having more sleep than she knew what to do with last night, she was tired. All the running and stress seemed to be finally catching up with her.

"I think I'll go take a shower and head to my room," she said without making eye contact with either of the two men. She couldn't afford to let Sean get a close look at her right now as tears pricked the backs of her eyes. Chin to chest, she coughed as cover before rushing upstairs as a tsunami of emotion threatened to slam into her. She vaguely heard something about fresh clothing in her size being folded on the bed for her. At least, that's what she thought she heard even though she had no idea who would have done this. Did they keep clothing around too?

A quick shower later, she was dressed in said clean clothes. She picked up her notebook and then her guitar. The song she'd been working on flooded her with more words and a melody.

She wasn't sure how long she'd been lost in thought when the soft knock at the door caught her attention.

"Come in," she said before Sean peeked his head inside.

"Everything okay?" he asked. The concerned wrinkles in his forehead melted her resolve.

"Sure," she said.

"That's not a definitive answer," he pointed out with a wink that melted her heart.

She couldn't help but smile despite recent events.

"You're welcome to come inside my room and sit down if you don't believe me," she said.

"Only if you'll play something for me," he stated. More of that melting took place.

"What do you want to hear?" she asked, always at a loss when someone asked her to play.

"Your favorite song," he said.

"That's always the one I'm working on in the moment," she said, then revised her comments by saying, "Unless it's giving me grief. Once I get over the hump and a song starts shaping into something, I'm the most excited about it."

Sean walked over to the foot of her bed and sat down, turning to face her. He was shirtless, fresh from the shower. She tried to look away from the scars on his chest and arms, his body a map of the battles he'd faced.

"I don't normally share music that I'm currently working on, but here goes." Raelynn took in a deep breath and started playing. Vocals came next. Nerves weren't normally something she'd battle with in a setting like this, except rejection from Sean would sting so much worse than if a random person was involved.

Then again, she didn't normally play for others until the song was finished.

Once she started singing, her hands slipped into muscle memory as she strummed the guitar. When she was finished, she dared to look over at Sean.

"That was incredible," he said with admiration that nearly knocked her off balance. She'd wanted him to like her music more than she'd wanted to admit.

As exhaustion set in, she bit back a yawn.

"I should go," he said.

"Would you stay?" she asked. "I won't sleep a whole day away again, but I haven't rested so well since this whole thing started and…"

She realized how selfish she probably sounded.

"But, you know, it's okay if you're more comfortable in the next room," she quickly added.

"I like being with you, Raelynn," he said, before

saying, "Makes my job easier in the long run if we're in the same place."

So much for falling down the rabbit hole of emotion with a comment like that one. It was the equivalent of a bucket of ice water being thrown over her head.

"I'd hate to make your job more difficult then," she quipped, wishing she could reel those words back in the second the snappy comment left her mouth.

She wasn't exactly certain what reaction she expected from Sean—anything but the one he gave. The corners of his lips upturned in a dry crack of a smile.

"I appreciate it," he said as he removed the guitar case from the bed, placing it in the corner instead. Next, he asked if he could help with the guitar.

"I've got it," she said, realizing she was far more tired than she imagined. She gently placed her beloved guitar back in its case before returning to a bed that was already occupied by Sean.

"Do you mind if I get comfortable?" he asked as she joined him on the bed.

"Be my guest," she said as a trill of awareness skittered across her skin, goose bumping her arms. Sean Hayes possessed a magnetism that was impossible to ignore. So, she didn't fight it. In times like these, she thought about HALT. Emotions were on edge when she was hungry, angry, lonely, or tired. In this case, she was tired. So, she chalked her emotions up to that as she climbed underneath the covers and tried to divert her gaze from Sean's muscled body.

He slipped out of his jeans, wearing only boxers, and she tried not to think about the thin layers of cotton between their bare naked skin.

Her breath caught in her throat and her mouth felt like she'd licked a glue stick. Since no one had ever made her feel this intensely, she decided to relax into it as much as possible without letting it catch her off guard too badly.

Before clicking off the light, she ran her finger along a two-inch scar on his right pec. "How did that happen?"

"Unfortunate knife fight," he said like he was reading the Sunday paper instead of talking about something that had left a permanent mark on his body.

"Who won?" she asked.

"I did," he said quickly, "or it would have been much worse.

She ran the tip of her finger along the raised and damaged skin. "I can't imagine how much this must have hurt as a knife was being stabbed at you."

"It's not as bad as you might think," he said.

"How?" she continued, unfazed by his nonchalant attitude. "There is no way on earth that didn't hurt."

"Adrenaline kicks in at some point," he said, cutting off the light and repositioning her so that she fit perfectly in the crook of his arm. She resisted the temptation to curl her body around his—for a few moments at least. Then, she gave in. There was no use fighting the comfort she found in his arms or the sense of belonging that was so new to her that she barely recognized it.

"It has to hurt eventually," she said.

"Yes, but by then doctors have given you enough drugs to manage the pain," he said with conviction.

"Somehow, I just don't see you as the kind of person who would take drugs to cover anything," she insisted. He seemed like the kind of guy who would smile at pain, and not look back.

"You're not wrong," he said, and she could feel his smile if not see it.

"Why not work on the ranch?" she asked. "You grew up there. You must have been familiar with the work."

"I was and I am," he said. "My family is being called back to discuss our roles there and I'm supposed to be on leave."

"It's terrible of me but I almost forgot you said you had somewhere else to be," she admitted. She'd been so wrapped up in her own case that she hadn't considered he had his own life.

"No worries," he said. "I haven't wanted to talk about it a whole lot to be honest."

"Why not?" she asked, figuring she'd pushed this far. Why not go all the way?

"There's a lot of history there with my grandfather who passed away not that long ago," he said after a long sigh.

"You didn't get along?" she asked.

"No one got along with the man as far as I know," he stated.

"You must be close with your siblings," she continued while they were on the subject of him. "And you were close with your mother, right?"

"Not as close as I probably should have been," he said. "I withdrew and dealt with losing my father at a young age all alone." He hesitated for a long moment. "I don't think my problems compare to what you've been through so I haven't made a big deal out of them. Suffice it to say, families can be complicated."

"Looking from the outside in, all I ever wanted was a family while growing up," she said. "I guess it never occurred to my young mind they might be complicated."

His chuckle was a low rumble in his chest. It was sexier than she wanted to acknowledge while snuggled up to his side.

"Isn't the grass always greener on the other side?" he commented.

"I guess so," she said. "Funny how that works, isn't it? I would have given anything to be part of a big family growing up, so much so that I used to fantasize about it all the time. Turns out, nothing is perfect."

"Nope, but there are things that are pretty darn close," he said with a low gravely quality to his tone. "Being here with you might not be under ideal circumstances, but I can't regret those bringing us together."

He spoke so softly that she barely heard him. And yet, he could have been screaming for the effect his words had on her. They traveled through her like stray lightning on a sunny day, awakening places that had been long since dormant.

“Getting to know you is the best thing that has come out of this,” she said quietly. Before things could go any further or she could say something she might wish she hadn’t, she closed her eyes and forced them to remain that way until sleep took her.

Chapter Fifteen

Breakfast the next morning came at five o'clock sharp. Sean had barely slept a wink, unable to shut down his thoughts on the case and, to be honest, the sizzling hot kisses he'd shared with Raelynn. His brain bounced back and forth, which was the reason he needed to ignore the attraction brewing between them. That had been impossible to do with her warm body curled around his side. Too many images of their legs and arms in a tangle in the sheets had slipped through his thoughts. What if he got distracted in a critical moment?

His eggs threatened to come back up at the thought of losing another person he cared about. Bile burned the back of his throat as he finished the dishes. Within fifteen minutes, they were in their vehicles ready to head out for the day.

"You've been quiet this morning," Raelynn said after buckling her seat belt.

"I've been focused on interview questions," he said, hearing the slight chill in his own voice. The way she stiffened said she felt it, too.

"Where are we going first?" she asked, barely masking what sounded like hurt in her tone.

"Rudy's house," he stated.

"Is it strange that I don't know where that is?" she asked, but he could tell the question was rhetorical.

"Red Oak," he supplied.

"Isn't that half an hour or so south of Dallas?"

"It's on the way to Ashley and Erik's place so I figured we'd kill two birds with one stone," he commented, gripping the steering wheel a little tighter as he navigated off the property and onto the road heading toward Interstate 35. Once there, Red Oak and Dallas would be a straight shot north.

"Good," she said. That one spoken word had the finality of death. A steel wall came up, and he tried to convince himself it was probably for the best. His feelings weren't hot and cold, despite the impression he was giving. The war going on inside told him that he needed to get a grip and keep it. The last thing he wanted was to send her mixed signals.

Sean barely got the SUV up to speed on the highway when his vehicle suddenly went into a spin. From the side-view mirror, he saw his tires skidding, jumping and rolling. Using both hands, he white-knuckled the steering wheel to maintain as much control as humanly possible. He eased his foot off the gas and forced himself not to stomp the brake. Either could cause a death roll.

Raelynn gasped but she didn't panic. He listened for the sounds of hard braking and crunching noises, hoping to minimize collateral damage.

There wasn't much he could do here except use physical force to regain steering and keep them from flipping. Using the driving skills he'd learned while in the military, he managed to straighten out the vehicle while he slowed down enough to pull off to the shoulder. He tapped the button on the dash to engage the emergency flashers and then immediately turned to Raelynn.

"Are you hurt anywhere?" he asked as he checked her over for blood. A flashback hit and suddenly he was back inside the Humvee in the desert, frantically dragging bodies out. He'd lost two best friends who were like brothers that day. Anger filled his chest.

"I'm okay." Raelynn's reassuring voice broke through the mental image. "I'm here. I think we lost a tire back there, but that's all." She brought her hands up to cup his face. Her touch brought focus and clarity to his mind. "I'm right here."

His pulse had jacked up through the roof and he needed to be reminded where he was and who was with him. He needed to get his feet back on the ground.

Sean had his military training to thank for always being prepared. Changing a tire on the side of the highway wasn't his smartest move with traffic zipping by at seventy-plus mile an hour speeds, except there was no choice. He set up cones and went to work fixing the tire. His next problem was big. There were no lug nuts. They'd gotten loose somehow and then, once he'd gotten the vehicle up to a decent speed, they'd failed. The scenario seemed a little too big of a coincidence.

The first thing he did was grab his phone. He fired off a text indicating that he needed assistance. The tremors made holding his cell a little harder to accomplish, but he pulled it off. Then he described the part he needed and why in a short message. In their business, a phone was pretty much all it took to get things moving while out in the field. He would be lost without his cell.

The missing lug nuts meant a delay. This scenario also meant he had to update Mitch.

"What happened out here?" Raelynn asked, joining him.

"I'm guessing sabotage," he stated, even though he had no idea how anyone could get on the compound to pull off anything close.

Raelynn gasped.

"How?" she asked.

"That's a good question," he said. "I was with you yesterday. As far as I know, there were only three of us at the compound recently. I'm certain Mitch is keeping it that way in order to keep you safe."

"Would I be in danger otherwise?" she asked.

"Under the circumstances, Mitch would go to whatever lengths necessary to ensure very few people knew about you and where you were," he said. She responded with a look that said she understood and appreciated the reasons behind Mitch's protection. This was personal to his boss, and he was doing everything in his power to protect her privacy.

Sean didn't like the fact they were stranded out in the open like this. It might be part of someone's plan to flush them out. He caught himself before instinctively reaching for her hand. Instead, he walked around to the side of the vehicle while nudging her along. She caught on fast, glancing around before following him. He stood close enough to cover her with his body should gunfire break out. Her back was against the passenger door. Her pulse thumped at the base of her neck.

"If someone can get on property, wouldn't they have just shot at us last night? Or on the way to our vehicle this morning?" she asked.

"I'm still trying to figure out how someone got past security at all," he admitted. "There are always holes but this? Tampering with one of our vehicles? It's unheard of."

"Is there any chance this was a random occurrence?" she asked. "Even a slim one?"

"Yes, of course," he stated. "Or someone realized they had to get in and out before they got caught—someone who might be familiar with our systems."

"That hints at someone who either works with you or would be in your line of work," she said.

"Drake," he said, confirming that he was likely thinking the same thing she was.

Sean issued a sharp sigh. His cell buzzed in his hand. Mitch's name came up on the screen.

"Everything okay out there?" Mitch asked immediately after Sean answered.

"So far, so good," Sean reassured him as he

watched out for any signs of a vehicle slowing down as cars and trucks zipped by. "We hit a little speed bump, though." He gave a quick rundown of what happened.

Mitch was quiet, thoughtful.

"Let me check into it," he said. "It might not be safe for the two of you to return until I can be assured there's no threat."

"Got it," Sean stated.

"I'd set something up for you, but it might be safer if you go dark on this one," Mitch said. They both knew why. If someone had broken into the system, as rare as that would be, Mitch's comms might be compromised.

"I got this," Sean reassured. "I see lights. I'm good."

They ended the call. The flashing light pattern meant help had arrived. A driver pulled behind them in a blue sport utility. A small brunette with a fierce expression exited the vehicle. She left the door open, walked to the back of Sean's truck and faced the road. Her right hand was tucked behind her leg, concealing the fact she was holding a Sig Sauer. A nod passed between her and Sean a second before she took her post. He recognized the agent who was there to swap vehicles so he and Raelynn could get on the road.

Sean walked Raelynn over to the passenger side of the vehicle before opening the door for her. He made certain she was safe as she claimed the seat. Next, he circled around the front of the vehicle scanning the area as he took the driver's seat.

The rest of the ride to Red Oak was church quiet. As much as Sean hated the silence between them, this was necessary. He needed to process what had just happened and his brain had locked on to one thought… Drake. Sean was being too closed-minded. Besides, there was always the off chance this had happened randomly. Vehicles failed. Parts gave out. It happened.

First stop, Rudy Cannon's place. Rudy lived in a small trailer park off the highway. Landscaping at the entrance was neatly kept and welcoming. The trailers were all newer models and in good condition. There was a small park with newer equipment and green grass across from the first trailer, which had a sign out front that read Property Manager. This person seemed to take pride in the small community, with rows of well-kept spaces and signs for upcoming events.

Rudy's was fourth on the right. A Chevy pickup was parked out front.

"That's his," she said. "Maybe I should text him and give him a heads-up that we're about to knock on his door."

"Maybe not," he said as she reached for her phone.

"Why?" she asked.

"I'd like to see his reaction to you showing up," he said. "He won't have time to prepare his responses, either. It'll tell me a whole lot more about him and the situation if he's caught off guard by your presence. His wife, too."

She nodded but didn't turn to look at him as he pulled up next to the Chevy. Before he could say much else, she hopped out of the vehicle and then slammed the door shut. To her credit, she waited for him to come around the front and join her before making a beeline toward the door.

"It's better if you're the one who does the knocking," he said to her. An apology died on his lips.

"Fine," she said—the one word people said when the exact opposite was true. She walked right up to the screen door, opened it, and then tapped three times.

A dark shadow passed over the peephole before the door swung open and an older gentleman stood in the frame. Surprise was a good word to describe his expression. The guy looked to be around five foot nine and had a skinny build. He was wiry, and those were always the unexpectedly strong ones. His once dark hair was now almost completely gray. He had on jeans and a Western shirt with a pack of cigarettes tucked inside the front pocket.

"Hi, Rudy," Raelynn started.

"Long time no see," Rudy responded with a nod of acknowledgment. His gaze bounced from Raelynn to Sean. "Come on in."

"Who is it?" a female voice called from behind him.

"Raelynn, and she brought company," Rudy explained as he stepped aside, ushering them in.

"This is Sean and he's a friend of mine," Rae-lynn said.

Rudy offered a handshake and, based on the man's grip strength, he was definitely stronger than he looked.

As they walked inside the double-wide, Sean got a good look at the room. There were a pair of leather recliners positioned to face a 52-inch flat-screen TV that sat on top of a particleboard stand. A woman pushed up from one of the recliners and silenced the TV with the remote.

"My wife, Blanch," Rudy said to Sean by way of introduction.

"Ma'am," Sean said.

"It's good to see you again, Blanch," Raelynn said.

"Same to you," Blanch responded. She wasn't more than five feet two inches tall and had on sweat-pants and a matching sweatshirt. She rubbed her hands down the front of her pants before offering them something to drink.

"No, thank you," Raelynn said as Rudy motioned toward the round table in the adjacent room. "We can't stay long," she continued.

"I'm hoping this visit is about getting back to work," Rudy stated. There were stacks of papers on top of most surfaces—*clutter* was a good word, bor-dering on *hoarders*. The place was clean, though. It was obvious someone had recently run a vacuum around and the linoleum flooring in the kitchen area had been washed.

"Soon," Raelynn promised. "I hope. I wanted to check on you and see how you were holding up."

"I'm anxious to be busy," he said, and his wife gave a slightly annoyed nod like she was ready for him to get back on the road, too.

The visit didn't take long for Sean to assess the situation and realize this person wasn't a threat. Neither was his wife. His gambling might be a problem. She would need to keep him away from petty cash while on tour. Other than that, he seemed like a decent person. Rudy had a beer in his hand. There were no additional signs of an alcohol problem, like empties lining the back of the kitchen sink or a trash bag full of crunched up cans. The place smelled like Febreze or a scented plug-in, not like stale beer.

All in all, the risk assessment here was low. One down, a couple to go.

RAELYNN KEPT QUIET after leaving Rudy's place. The conversation had been short. Sean had given his impression as soon as they left and were safely away from Rudy's home. In the end, she was right about her stage manager.

Her mind shifted gears as Sean navigated back onto Interstate 35. Anton Miles. The name wasn't familiar. Maybe he was the stalker. Maybe he was the one who'd been torturing her. Maybe he was the one who'd tried to kill her. But how did he end up being killed in the process?

"Do you know if Anton Miles's body was dumped

near my campsite or if he was killed right there?" she asked.

"That's a question for Mitch," Sean said. "He is heading up that part of the investigation."

"If this Drake character was behind all this, why kill Anton?" she asked.

"I still haven't figured that one out for myself," he admitted. "It would be nice if the coroner's report was back. That can take a few days depending on how backed up he is."

TV had ruined her for investigations like these. They made it seem like someone snapped a finger or "pulled rank" and got information within hours, when in reality it probably took days or weeks, if not months.

"I'm guessing Mitch has to wait just like everyone else," she said.

"For the most part, yes," he admitted. "There are times when he has a play to get something done earlier, but I haven't heard anything from him yet so I'm guessing that's not the case this time."

"It's only been a few hours since we left this morning," she added. There was something else on her mind, having to do with paternity. "Did you see the test results?"

He didn't look away from the road, but she could see his confusion from the side.

"DNA," she clarified.

"From last night?" he asked, then said, "No. It's none of my business."

Raelynn almost asked him what she'd done overnight to frustrate him because he'd been acting different all day. He'd seemed into the kisses they'd shared on the swing last night as much as she'd been, and there'd been no disagreement between them, so she didn't know what she'd done to cause the mood change.

Right now, though, she didn't have the time or energy to dissect it—might be best to roll with it and do her best not to let the rejection stab her in the chest.

"Did you want to know for yourself?" he asked.

"I didn't think I would ever want to," she admitted.

"What changed?" he asked.

"I'm not sure," she said. "Truth be told, I didn't think I'd change my mind about taking the darn thing, either. Yet now that the information is out there, I'm leaning toward wanting to know."

"I would imagine it's basic human nature to want to know where you came from," he said after a thoughtful pause. "No one would blame you for changing your mind about being told the results."

Before she could respond, he pulled in front of a concrete-and-glass building in North Dallas. The construction itself wasn't huge. Dallas wasn't a city of skyscrapers, so the outskirts were even less so. There were plenty of family neighborhoods and ten- to fifteen-story buildings. There were enough parks around that were filled with various youth soccer and baseball teams. Football was the kingpin sport in Texas.

Sean parked.

"I've never been one to flip-flop on a topic before," Raelynn admitted. "This is new territory for me."

"Everyone is allowed to change their mind," he said with a voice that soothed. For a second, she thought he might reach over to link their fingers like he'd done before, but the wall that had come up between them seemed to create a barrier he couldn't break through.

"I guess so," she said, not liking this middle ground between wanting to know if Mitch was her father and having a deep-seated desire for answers. Being taken back to reliving all those childhood fantasies that had turned out to be soul crushing wasn't her idea of how she wanted to spend her day.

Still. There it was. She could stick her head in the sand, or she could face possible disappointment again. Either way felt like a loss. Since she had no answers there, she figured they may as well try to find answers with Erik and Ashley Bradshaw.

Chapter Sixteen

Sean hung back as he followed Raelynn into the office building of Erik and Ashley Bradshaw. The slick, black-tile flooring and expansive fountain gave the place an untouchable opulence. This was definitely not Sean's taste, but he recognized the high-quality and high-cost materials as Raelynn walked toward the bar counter–height security desk.

Two men sat there watching computer screens. Both wore all-white, crisp uniforms. One of the men looked up at her.

"Name?" he asked. This guy looked to be in his early twenties—still wet behind the ears as far as Sean was concerned. And yet, he did his best to look threatening. Fresh-from-the-gym-but-never-tried-in-a-true-fight muscles bulged from underneath his short-sleeved uniform shirt. The guy had dark hair and pockmarks on his face from a serious teenage acne problem that was never adequately addressed.

"Raelynn Simmons," she said to him.

Recognition seemed to dawn at that point as Pockmarks nodded appreciatively.

"One moment please. I'll let Erik know you're here," Pockmarks said. Interesting that Pockmarks assumed she was there to see Erik. A twinge of jealousy struck that Sean had no right to. He needed to keep things in perspective. Ashley might feel the same way. After all, her husband was the one security seemed to think Raelynn was here to see. Were their meetings a normal, everyday thing?

He didn't like it for reasons he had didn't want to explain.

"Thank you," Raelynn said.

The second security guard barely looked up, but he wasn't glued to the screen in front of him that vacillated between various views of the building. Instead, he focused on a football game that was playing on his cell phone. He'd positioned it so that it looked like he was watching the other screen.

Lazy security was one of those fingernails-on-a-chalkboard situations for Sean.

Pockmarks—Lance, based on his name tag—told them to go on up a few seconds later.

The offices of Erik and Ashley Bradshaw were as over-the-top as the lobby downstairs—even more so, if at all possible. But it was the desk in Erik's office that gave away his insecurities. The mahogany furniture was bigger than any desk needed to be now that so many people worked on laptops. The executive chair was tall, whereas the others were shorter, giving the illusion of authority.

"Raelynn," Erik said as he pushed up to standing

from the behind the massive desk. "What an unexpected surprise."

Erik's gaze shifted from Raelynn to Sean, where it lingered. Question marks danced in the man's eyes, and Sean didn't like this scenario one bit.

"Hey, Erik," she said, without giving away any of her emotions. "Thought I'd stop by and see how you and Ashley were doing."

Erik made a show of coming around his desk and giving Raelynn a big, fake hug. "We're good. Just worried about you."

"How's Ashley?" Raelynn asked after breaking free.

Erik's gaze landed hard on Sean. The man seemed smart enough not to ask too many questions after Sean was introduced as Raelynn's friend.

"She's good," Erik said. "In fact, she'll be happy to see you."

Somehow, Sean doubted it.

"Let me buzz her in," Erik offered.

The woman who bounced into the room after the call was made reminded him of a former high school cheerleader. She was a blonde with fake lashes and other surgically enhanced features. She bopped into the room like she owned the place, even though it was her husband who probably did.

"Hey, Raelynn," Ashley said before leaning into a cheek-to-cheek fake hug. Her gaze zeroed in on Sean next. "Who is this?"

There was something about the way she spoke

that made him want to take a shower to clean off the grime.

"This is my friend Sean," Raelynn said, and he thought he saw something in her eyes. Jealousy?

Jealousy would be a major reason to get rid of Raelynn. What could Ashley gain from scaring Raelynn, though? Weren't her and her husband's finances tied to Raelynn doing well on the tour? Hadn't they bet on her like she was some kind of horse in the derby with high stakes? Did they see her as the long shot?

Sean's instinct was to get Raelynn as far away from these people as possible.

"Well, hello," Ashley said, going in for a hug that made Sean cringe. He wasn't certain if this type of person rankled him or if he was being overly dramatic. But the jealousy he saw in Ashley's eyes when she looked at Raelynn was unmistakable.

The couple went on the list of possible suspects. They weren't the type to get their hands dirty, though. No. These two would hide behind hiring someone to do the dirty work for them. Erik seemed fidgety, which wasn't helping Sean's impression of the guy. They had something to hide or cover all right. But what?

The real question was whether or not either one of them was capable of murder. What would they have to gain? Raelynn had been right in asking the question earlier. Sean still didn't have an answer to that one, no matter how much he racked his brain thinking about it. And he was digging deep to find answers to the question.

On the surface, they had everything to benefit from by keeping Raelynn on the tour. So why did he get such a creepy feeling around them? Creepy didn't automatically mean deadly. It seemed like a good idea to remind himself of that.

"DOES THIS VISIT mean you're going back on tour?" Ashley asked. Erik shot a look that Raelynn couldn't quite put her finger on.

"Not yet," Raelynn responded. "The stalker hasn't been caught, so it still isn't safe."

Ashley's gaze dropped to the floor for a second before bouncing back up. "Oh. Well. That's a shame. We were obviously hoping for better news when we saw you."

"I hope this isn't putting you guys in too bad of a position," Raelynn said. She could acknowledge that her stepping off the tour could impact their business.

"What can we do to help?" Erik asked with a smile that looked a little stiff and forced. He motioned for them to sit down.

Raelynn politely declined. The air in the room was…awkward, for lack of a better word. She'd surprised them by the visit. Why did they seem so uncomfortable? And nervous?

Sean came to mind. The way Erik kept glancing over at the man who dwarfed him caused her to believe Erik was threatened by Sean. Erik didn't come around the desk, either. The big hunk of mahogany seemed like a barrier to keep Sean from coming at Erik, which made no sense until she glanced back at Sean. He stood in the doorway, arms crossed, leaning against the jamb and blocking out all the light from the hallway. His physical presence could be overwhelming at first—she remembered from their first meeting. Over the course of a couple of days, she'd adjusted to it. She said *adjusted* because one could never get used to someone Sean's imposing size. When he walked into a room, she would bet women smiled and men straightened up a little, keeping one eye on the most alpha person there. He took up space in a way that was difficult to describe and impossible to duplicate.

Erik noticed. He kept a weary-looking eye on Sean.

"Nothing much," Raelynn said to answer Erik's question. "I just wanted to stop by in person so you could see that I'm still alive and kicking. We're working with authorities to figure out who my stalker is, and I hope to be back on tour in a matter of days." She wasn't exactly certain what had possessed her to lie, except she was running on instinct at this point while trying to feel out the room.

Ashley's gaze widened with the word *authorities*. Once again, Raelynn couldn't quite pinpoint the reaction.

"We're so glad you stopped by," Ashley said, seeming to recover from her...shock? Yes, the emotion had definitely been shock and a little bit of fear, too. Interesting.

Ashley moved toward the door but Sean didn't budge.

"I have a question before we go," he said, staring Erik down like Sean was a bull before the charge and Erik waved a red flag.

"What can we do for you?" Erik asked with a hint of shakiness in his voice.

"Tell me how your business is doing," Sean said. The authority in his voice would make it impossible to ignore or get out of answering.

"Great," Ashley said in a voice that almost shook. The normally confident-to-the-point-of-almost-obnoxious blonde's smile faltered. It was just a split second but spoke volumes.

Had they overextended themselves in financing Raelynn's tour? They were a small business with a few interests, not a huge conglomerate or record label. Those had deep pockets. This was a family affair. Had they been hoping to hit a home run with her tour this year? The last couple of years, they'd made a small profit, or at least they'd said so. Would they have reason to lie?

Sean seemed satisfied with the answer. He thanked them for their time and then asked Raelynn if she was ready to go.

"Keep in touch with us," Ashley said. She glanced over at her husband. "Do you have Raelynn's new cell number? The old one seems to have canceled service, which was probably because of the situation with the stalker."

"I have to keep this one private, for now," Raelynn

hedged, not wanting to give out this number in case they could track it. "The authorities said something about a chip and locator. I'm not supposed to give out the number."

"We understand," Ashley said, twisting her fingers together in a knot. She compressed her lips and then forced a smile. "Your safety is all we care about."

Really? It didn't seem like it a minute ago when Ashley was urging Raelynn to get back on the tour before her stalker was caught.

"Keep us posted on any leads the law comes up with," Erik said. Ashley whirled around and clapped her hands together.

"Yes, do that," she said with a little too much enthusiasm.

"You bet," Raelynn said before promising to call soon.

Sean stepped aside into the hallway and held a hand out, indicating she should go first. There was a lot of comfort walking out of that office, knowing someone had her back.

"We should wait to talk until we get on the road," Sean said the minute they were buckled in and the engine hummed.

She nodded, thinking that she wouldn't want to do any of this without him. He'd been a lifeline.

Once they were out of the parking lot and the building disappeared, he shook his head.

"They're hiding something," he said, pulling into

the parking lot of a fast-food restaurant. "I want to know what it is."

He parked and then fished his cell phone out of his pocket. He fired off a text on that magic phone of his that made SUVs appear out of thin air and who knew what else.

"It'll take her a little while before she can get into the system," he said.

"What did you think of the look Erik gave his wife when I said I wasn't going back on tour?" she asked, breaking the sudden silence.

"He looked guilty as hell of something," he said.

"Ashley was nervous," Raelynn pointed out. "She's always had a bigger-than-Texas personality, the kind you think is the norm if you're not from around here."

"Along with the tumbleweeds rolling down the streets in every major city," he said with a smirk, and it was the first break in tension.

"Why do people from other states still think that?" she said with a laugh. "I'll give you the fact we have more real cowboys than most. And, yes, we bump into them just about everywhere. And small towns are quaint. Texans are quirky. Some women think bleached blond is the only way to go with hair. But that's not the majority. Some of us have red hair. A whole lot are brunettes."

"We come in a wide variety of packages," he agreed. "Some things are consistent, though."

"Opening doors for women," she said.

"Unless they don't want it," he stated. "We adapt."

"Yes, we do," she agreed. "Or we stop all growth."

"Which is basically the definition of dying," he said.

The last word sent a cold shiver racing down her spine. Were Ashley and Erik after her? Once again, she had to wonder why they would be. They both acted strangely in the office.

"When I think back, Erik did make me uncomfortable when we first signed," she said. "In fact, I almost refused to sign the papers because his hand dropped to my backside when we stood behind a podium together announcing the deal was being hammered out."

"Did you confront the bastard?" Sean's dark tone would make a professional fighter nervous.

"Yes," she said. "He apologized and said it was an accident. I told him that it made me uncomfortable and if it ever happened again, accident or not, I would cut his fingers off."

Sean's grin was almost ear to ear.

"That was a good response," he said with a chuckle and more than a hint of admiration.

"It seemed appropriate at the time," she said, laughing. Now that she thought about it, she'd definitely drawn a line in the sand when it came to sexual harassment.

"He had all his fingers, so I'm guessing he heard you loud and clear," Sean mused. Then his expression morphed to a serious one. "He didn't cross that line but I'm wondering how he talked about you to his wife. Did he pay special attention to you when you were together?"

"I'm not sure I'd classify it as *special*, but he did stick to my side," she said. "I guess I just thought it was part of the sponsorship. He would talk me up when they visited us on tour—that kind of thing, like any promotor would."

"Or someone who cared more than he wanted to let on," Sean pointed out.

The words resonated more than she wanted them to. Any married person, woman or man, would be jealous if their partner became interested in someone else. Interested to the point of stalking?

Chapter Seventeen

At least Rudy and his wife could be crossed off the suspect list in Sean's view. He'd take all the progress they could get. In the back of his mind, his brain was still trying to work out how Ashley or Erik could have penetrated home base with all the security there.

Vehicles failed, though. They weren't like airplanes where a mechanic meticulously worked through a punch list before every flight to ensure every component was ready for the trip.

At this point, he set those thoughts aside.

"Mitch doesn't want us coming back to headquarters," he said to Raelynn, who'd become quiet. The revelation Erik could be her stalker seemed to strike hard. Sean made a mental note to ask his hacker to get a copy of Erik's calendar to see if dates matched up. He would also need to get a list of dates from Raelynn about when she'd felt threatened.

"Should I look up a hotel or do you have something else in mind?" she asked with a detached quality to her voice.

"My first thought was a safe house since I didn't want either of our credit cards on file anywhere," he said.

"But you decided against it?" she asked.

"Yes." They could find a place to hide in plain sight—like downtown Dallas, or his family-owned property in various places around Texas. Since Sean had to assume the worst-case scenario, he couldn't risk someone making the connection to his family name. If someone was smart enough to breach the compound without leaving a trace, they might know who Sean was. Another thought bugged him. Why make the wreck look like an accident? The first thought that popped into his brain had to do with Drake.

"What did you have in mind, then?" she asked.

"I have a buddy who is still active duty," he said, thinking out loud. "I could probably shoot him a text. He keeps a townhouse in Dallas, where he's from. Says coming back to it and being part of the city keeps him connected to home."

"Doesn't sound like anyone could connect us to his place," she said.

"Do you mind?" he asked, handing over the phone before banking a U-turn. He'd unlocked his cell a second before the switch.

"What am I doing?" she asked after taking the offering.

"Pull up a contact by the name of Cash," he said. "His first name is Joseph but we all called him Cash."

"Is that his last name?" she asked absently as she focused on the task.

"No," he said with a grin. "The man refuses to use a credit card, so we had to make sure he had enough local currency to buy something every time we went into town."

Her laugh had a musical quality.

"It gets worse," he continued. "That wasn't enough to earn him the nickname. Cash thought the government was tracking everyone through the chip in their credit cards. He had a level of paranoia that makes us laugh to this day."

"Didn't he technically work for the government?" she asked as she sent the message.

"Still does," Sean said. "That's what makes it so funny."

"Sounds like you guys like to give him a hard time," she said, scrolling. "I found his contact information. What do you want me to say?"

"Ask if we can use his place," he said.

She did.

A response dinged almost immediately.

"He said we're good to go," she stated. "I wish I'd brought clothes with me, though."

"We can stop off at a store so you can pick up whatever you need on the way," he said. "I can't promise anything fancy, but it'll get the job done."

"All I need is a few items to get by over the next few days," she said.

"It occurred to me that my ready bag is still in my other vehicle. I'll need a few supplies, as well," he realized. Cash would have shampoo, razors and essentials in his apartment. Since his friend was four inches shorter than Sean, borrowing clothes wouldn't work. Plus, they would need food. He doubted there'd be anything but cans. Anything else would go bad while Cash was away for such long periods of time.

"Where are we headed?" she asked.

"Henderson Avenue area?" he confirmed. "Cash's place is right off Henderson."

She pulled out her phone. "Looks like we should head a little bit north if we want to find a superstore for shopping."

"Tell me which way to go," he said.

It took a little less than an hour to get squared away. Cash's place was technically a town house, not an apartment, near Garrett Park by Bryan Parkway. Sean pulled around to the garage at the back of the three-story town house. Leaving the driver's side door open, he zipped out and punched in the code on the keypad to open the two-car garage. He used the same one from past visits and it worked.

He parked next to Cash's prized Harley-Davidson motorcycle, which had been granted an entire space. The SUV spilled over into the spot by approximately a foot, so it all worked out.

Sean opened the hatch and they unloaded supplies together until the back was empty. He made the final trip downstairs to the garage to close up. Scanning the area for anyone or anything out of the ordinary, he breathed a sigh of relief as he realized no one had followed them or seemed particularly interested in what was going on. Good. It was possible they could set up here for a couple of days until information started rolling in.

By the time he returned to the middle floor comprised of the kitchen, dining and living areas, Raelynn had put away most of the food and drink items.

"Your clothing bags are those," she said, pointing to the couple of bulging bags on the end of the granite counter that divided the living spaces. The island was large enough to sit at and eat, and there were barstools for that purpose. There was no need for a dining table. Instead, Cash had a regulation size pool table in the center of the room. Farther in, there was a leather couch and a TV affixed to the wall above the fireplace, along with a wall of windows straight ahead. Being on the second floor, he wasn't too worried about keeping the blinds closed at all times. In fact, it might look suspicious if they were. Nighttime was a different story and it would be getting dark soon.

Sean was familiar with the layout. On the third story, there were two bedrooms and an office. An outside spiral staircase affixed to the balcony led to a rooftop deck. It offered a good vantage point and could be used strategically to monitor the area. A small laundry room was down on the first floor in the garage area.

"I'll show you to your bedroom whenever you're ready," he said to Raelynn.

"Okay," she said, but she was already familiarizing herself with the layout of the kitchen. She'd located a decent chopping knife and a good-sized serving bowl. Romaine lettuce and veggies were on the block in a heartbeat, pieces being tossed inside the bowl or in her mouth. She worked quickly and efficiently. Thinking about how sweet those lips tasted wasn't good for the whole "keeping his distance" stance.

A pot of water came to boiling on the stove behind her.

"Do you want me to throw in the spaghetti?" he asked, moving next to her, almost back-to-back.

"Sure," she said. "The sauce needs to go on, too. Can you do that while I finish the salad?"

"You got it," he said, liking the way they worked together a little more than he wanted to admit or acknowledge. His backing off rule might prove more difficult than he'd expected.

RAELYNN FINISHED THE salad and then moved one of the barstools so they could see each other when they talked over dinner, rather than being side by side and looking at the stove. A few minutes later, they were seated and having dinner.

"The only thing that could make this dinner better would be a glass of wine to go with it," she said. "But it's important to keep a clear head."

"Same reason I didn't pick up any beer," he said. "I don't drink while I'm working."

Those last words hit like harpoons. They shouldn't. He was working, as well as doing his boss a favor by watching over his potential daughter.

"Water works," she said, retrieving a glass and filling it from the sink. "Do you want anything?"

"No, thanks," he responded. "I'll brew coffee after dinner. It'll be fine."

"This might sound like a weird request," she began, "because I know we need to keep at it until we crack this nut. Mentally, I'm exhausted. All I want to do is check out for one night on the couch and do something normal like watch a movie. You don't have to join me if you don't—"

"I'll do it," he said. "There's a little convenience store on the corner a couple blocks away."

"We passed right by it," she said.

"I can run out and get wine if that sounds better than coffee," he offered, nodding. The fact he was willing to set aside all the heaviness of the day so she could get a mental break meant the world to her.

"Only if it won't take too much away from the case. I know it's important," she said.

"A few hours won't hurt anything," he quickly stated. "Plus, you never know—a break might be just what we both need to be able to come at this fresh in the morning. It's been one helluva day."

"I'll grab a quick shower while you run out," she said, finishing off the best sit-down meal she'd had in far too long.

Raelynn exhaled. Really exhaled. She'd been on the move for months now. The stalker had been around longer, several months of worry and double-checking what might be lurking in the shadows.

"Go ahead and shower while I clean up the dishes.

Take the bigger room," he said. There wasn't much sexier than a self-sufficient man. Sean had the looks, too. Between those intense honey-brown eyes that seemed to look right through her and a carved-from-granite jawline, he was sex in a bucket. Some people seemed to get it all. Sean Hayes was one of them. After several kisses that had lit a dozen sizzling fires inside her, she was starting to have those ridiculous fantasies again—the ones that involved having a big family. Since she felt burned every time the two of them started to get close, she decided to stop touching the fire, no matter how tempting the flame might be.

Raelynn excused herself, grabbed her bags and headed up the stairs. She checked out the rooms on the third floor. The main bedroom was across the hallway from an office. Toward the back was a guest room complete with a full bathroom. She put her stuff in the guest room and then headed toward the bathroom, thinking it would be easier if she kept some separation between them.

Besides, she was being strategic, because someone would have to walk right past the door of the bedroom where Sean was sleeping to get to her. Based on what she'd witnessed so far, it was the way he would most likely set things up if he was on a protection detail. It dawned on her that he might be putting up a wall because of what had happened in the past. He'd told her that he didn't do protection details any longer, and here he'd been thrown into this one. To be fair, he was the one who'd committed to it after feeling like he'd brought danger to her doorstep at Hamilton Pool Preserve. A few days had passed, even though it felt like weeks ago.

She showered, changed into fresh clothes and then headed downstairs. The thought of a normal night was almost too good to be true. Adrenaline bursts throughout the day had drained her, and she wanted nothing more than to sink into the couch and find a good show to watch.

The minute she stepped on the last stair, Sean said he'd be right back. He disappeared before she saw him. The dishes were all done, though. Having the first real dinner in weeks and a shower made her feel half human again, and like she might not live in this nightmare forever.

The floor vibrated from the garage door opening and then closing. She hunted around for the remote and found it along with a couple of folded blankets in a basket underneath the coffee table. The blankets were several shapes, sizes, colors and textures. She tossed a couple onto the couch and then clicked the power button on the remote.

The TV sprang to life, and she felt a sense of accomplishment.

Fifteen minutes passed when she heard a creak sound upstairs. Her pulse galloped. Raelynn jumped up and immediately set the remote down. She glanced around, searching for something to use as a weapon. There was nothing heavy or blunt to use in the living room. Going to the kitchen meant passing the stairwell.

Another creak had her feet moving. She didn't have a whole lot of time to reason this out if there was a threat in the house. It was dark outside, so she cut off the lights as she moved through the rooms, passing around the back side of the pool table. This level of the house didn't have an exit other than a Juliet balcony. Did the doors even open or were they more for show?

Rather than risk it, she stayed on the path toward the kitchen. The last light being turned off plunged her into darkness. Her eyes would take time to adjust—time she didn't have as another creak sounded.

Houses settled. Was this normal or something to be concerned about? The wind was picking up outside, too. She might be panicking over nothing. Was this what her life was going to be like now? Afraid of every unexpected sound?

She felt around on the granite counter, searching for the block with all the knives and sharp kitchen scissors. Her phone was in her room, so there was no time to grab it. She found the handle of the knife as the hum of the garage vibrated underneath her feet. Relief flooded her as she immediately heard the garage door go down again. Sean was inside the town house, at least.

The creaking noises stopped. Of course they did. She flipped on the light. She kept hold of the carving knife, gripping the handle tightly just in case an intruder was standing still and, therefore, not making a sound. The person could be waiting for the right opportunity to strike.

Sean appeared next to her out of nowhere, disarming the knife as he put his other hand over her mouth to muffle her scream. A battlefield of electrical impulses assaulted her as she felt his warm breath against the nape of her neck.

In the next moment, he vanished up the stairs. Meanwhile, she was still trying to catch her breath and calm her racing pulse. It was shocking how quickly he'd disarmed her, and the scenario taught her a lesson about being prepared for anything. The knife she'd wielded could have very well been used against her.

Sean returned a few moments later, walking down the stairs without seeming worried about how much noise he made.

"What happened?" he asked before retrieving bags that he'd set down by the door leading to the garage.

"I heard creaking sounds coming from upstairs," she said, feeling like she'd just panicked in the biggest way possible. Embarrassment heated her cheeks. "I'm sorry. I think I just overreacted."

"Don't be," he said like it was nothing. He had a unique ability to make her feel better no matter the circumstances—even when her emotions got the best of her, which didn't used to happen in her old world before the stalker. Being around Sean gave her the feeling she could conquer all of her fears and insecurities. It wasn't something she'd experienced often in her thirty-one years on this earth.

Almost thirty-one. Was the number part of the

reason she was suddenly thinking about having a big family someday? Did she have some sort of internal clock ticking that was waking up? Raelynn had never considered herself one of those people who would wake up and suddenly crave kids. And she didn't. Not right now, at least. But then, she hadn't allowed herself to think about being part of a big family since she was five years old and one of her new 'siblings' beat the living daylights out of Raelynn for crying herself to sleep after another disappointing adoption day.

"It's okay upstairs," Sean reassured. "I checked every window and possible entry point. It's all good."

Raelynn exhaled the breath she'd been holding.

"Are you sure?" she asked.

"One hundred percent," he stated. "We can set the alarm, even though Cash never does when he's away. Sometimes he has someone check on the place and doesn't want the hassle of the City of Dallas coming down hard on him for false alarms."

"More of the government watching over him?" she mused, even though nothing felt funny right now.

"Something like that," he said with a chuckle. He studied her for a long moment and she'd never felt stripped so bare. "Do you want to watch that movie now?"

"Yes," she said, grateful he didn't ask her if she wanted to talk about it more. As much as she might wish Sean would spend the night with her again, she wouldn't ask. A movie? She could do that.

Chapter Eighteen

Every instinct Sean possessed had kicked in when he'd seen all the lights off at Cash's house. He'd cursed himself for leaving Raelynn alone, vulnerable. Finding her with a knife in her hand, ready to face whatever came her way, had shown him that she wasn't going to wait around for someone to save her when she was capable of fighting back. He respected the hell out of her for it.

"Do you have a preference on movies?" she asked as he poured a glass of wine for her.

"Something with action," he responded.

"How about comedy?" she asked as he opened a bottle of beer. Before joining her with the drinks, he set the alarm.

"Comedy's good," he stated, sensing she needed something light after such a heavy few days. If she was freaking out over settlement noise or wind, she wasn't in a good place. He of all people knew what it was like. Coming back from the military with PTSD and nowhere to land had had him ready to jump out of his skin when a cat walked past the window. The motion had sent him to a dark place. Forget about Fourth of July fireworks—those sent him into a complete spiral as he dropped to all fours.

So, yeah, she was doing a whole lot better than him after a traumatic experience.

"What do you think about this one?" she asked as a comedy special filled the screen.

"Looks good to me," he said before grabbing the bag of popped popcorn from the convenience store and joining her with full arms. He was pretty sure this was the comedian who'd recently fathered a child right after his release from rehab. The special was dated a couple of years prior, before the meltdown. Shame, he thought. The guy had been married to someone else the year prior to his rehab stint. At least he was getting help.

Sean settled on the couch next to Raelynn. There was something about physical contact with her that made him relax, that calmed his overactive nervous system.

Sitting there, being on the couch with her next to him about to watch a comedy special, righted everything in his world. He also realized in that instant she had the power to shred his world. And, this time, he couldn't care less.

The comedian was funny, and Raelynn seemed able to let her guard down enough to enjoy the set. Sean, however, couldn't stop his mind from racing, not even with a beer that was meant to help him relax. Thoughts were on a hamster wheel, churning round and round, and he was unable to slow them, let alone stop them.

The noises earlier had sent her into panic mode. He didn't like the idea of her walking around scared all the time. If anything happened to her…

Sean couldn't go there, not even hypothetically. Ignoring logic as he set everything on the counter, he reached for her and then tugged her over to his side of the couch. She was resistant at first, which stabbed him in the center of the chest.

This time, she didn't lean her head on his shoulder or curl her body around his. She didn't relax into him. She did, however, let her outer thigh rest against his. He'd take it. Sean had never needed anyone in his life, so the desire burning a hole through his chest was foreign. He felt the disappointment, that by pushing her away he'd accomplished the goal a little too well. That one was on him, and he couldn't go back and change it now without coming across as wishy-washy.

Three-quarters of the way through the show, she relaxed a little more. At one point, she turned on to her side and grabbed a pillow to hug against her chest as something niggled at the back of Sean's mind. Since overly focusing on it wouldn't help, he forced his thoughts in a different direction.

A small burst of pride filled his chest that he was able to give Raelynn a night of normal, as she'd called it. She deserved this and so much more. Sean was slowly coming to the realization that he wanted to be the one to give it to her.

With her background, gaining her trust wouldn't be easy. She would be worth the effort, though.

Figuring they needed to get some shut-eye tonight, he excused himself to take a shower when there were about fifteen minutes of the show remaining. Once upstairs, he headed into the main bedroom to find his bags sitting on the bed. There was no sign of Raelynn's things. He checked the adjoining bathroom next. Nothing in there, either.

He headed over to the guest room. The fact she'd set up inside shouldn't feel like a sucker punch to the solar plexus the way it did. There wasn't much he could do about it now. Besides, he didn't need much sleep and he'd gotten more than enough over the past few nights. Normally on a mission he'd grab a couple of minutes here and there, enough to keep his brain's battery charged. Long periods of concentration were good for research and problem-solving, as long as he didn't stay on one challenge for too long. This would give him a chance to look at the situation from different angles to see if he could get a little deeper.

Sean should check in with the boss, too. Not hearing from Mitch wasn't exactly a bad thing—although, after what had happened with the lug nut, he had a heightened concern for Mitch's safety. This was a good reason to break the request to go dark. If Drake was coming at Mitch, there was no telling the lengths to which the man would go.

Which circled Sean's thoughts back to Raelynn and the possibility she was Mitch's daughter. An argument could be made for him asking for the test results in the best interests of the case. But knowing before Raelynn seemed wrong. Sean was good at hiding things, but she might pick up on the shift in direction of the case and that would give her information she didn't want.

Complicated didn't begin to describe the situation. *Messy* was probably a better word.

Showered, shaved and feeling human again in pants with no shirt, Sean headed downstairs. Raelynn was curled up on the couch. The steady rise and fall of her chest signaled she'd fallen asleep. He didn't want to disturb her, so he placed a blanket over her before grabbing his laptop and setting up at the granite island in the kitchen. He positioned the barstool so that he could see both rooms, the stairwell leading upstairs and the door leading down a flight of stairs to the garage.

He picked up his cell phone and fired off a message to Mitch to see how he was doing. A thumbs-up response came a few seconds later, much to Sean's relief. Since that was the extent of their communication, Sean figured there was no news to report.

Scrolling through his texts, he stopped on one that had come in from his tech guru while he was in the shower. Matrix was her code name, and all he needed to know about her. The message told him to check his email. Now he was finally getting somewhere.

On the laptop, he pulled up his account, then scanned for Matrix's note. There wasn't a whole lot to scroll through, considering few people had knowledge of this account. The message had several attachments. One by one he read through them.

"What time is it?" Raelynn asked as he read the last page of the very last file. She stretched her arms out and yawned.

Sean glanced at the clock on the computer screen. "Two thirty."

"Wow," she said, sitting up. "With all the sleep I'm getting, I'll be normal in no time."

"Are you up for a while or headed upstairs?" he asked, figuring he could put on a pot of coffee if she wanted a cup. It was about time he stood up and stretched anyway. Plus, if she wasn't tired, he could give her an update. She needed to hear what he'd found out about her backers.

"Definitely awake," she said.

"Hungry?" he asked.

"I'm still full from dinner," she said as she pushed up to standing and then made her way across the room to join him at the granite island.

"Coffee?" he asked, as he was already in the process of pulling everything together for a pot. Cash had supplies, but they hadn't taken any chances, so there was more than enough to go around.

"Now, that sounds amazing even though it's late," she said. "I'll be right back."

She dashed upstairs with a smile on her face that was about to be ripped to shreds when he told her about Ashley and Erik. Sean bit back a curse.

Raelynn needed to know what Matrix had uncovered.

SEAN HAD A look in his eyes that told Raelynn something was different. Her first thought was that he had knowledge as to whether or not Mitch was her father and was having a difficult time hiding the fact. Her pulse raced as she rejoined him at the island after splashing water on her face and brushing her teeth upstairs.

The first sip of coffee made a dent in helping her clear the rest of the cobwebs. Not even a few calming breaths could settle her nerves. So, she went for it. “What’s going on?”

Sean nodded, took a sip of fresh brew and then leaned forward.

“I got a report back from Matrix,” he said. She must have given quite the look because he added, “From tech.”

“Oh,” she said, drawing out the word and exhaling at the same time.

It was his turn to look confused.

“What did you think I was about to tell you?” he asked, studying her. Before she could respond, it seemed to dawn on him what she might be referring to. He shot a look of apology before shaking his head. “I don’t have any knowledge as to the results.” He didn’t look away and the room heated underneath his stare. “If you have questions or wanted to change your mind, it’s not too late.”

“Mitch probably doesn’t have confirmation yet, so it would be working myself up for nothing at this point,” she reasoned. A growing part of her wanted to know, but she wasn’t ready to handle more disappointment. *Possible disappointment*, an annoying voice in the back of her mind pointed out. An argument could be made for her being disappointed either way. If the answer turned out to be not a match, there would be sadness at this point. If the opposite was true, Raelynn would never know her mother.

Sean reached across the island and covered her hand with his. Warmth spiraled through her and her breath caught in her throat. This man had an effect on her like no other. She cleared her throat trying to ease the sudden dryness.

After taking a sip of coffee, she said, "You have news from Matrix."

"Yes," he said. "I'm afraid you're not going to like it."

"Ashley and Erik are working together?" she asked.

"Not exactly," he stated. "Turns out their finances are in trouble. Erik hasn't been paying vendors in some of their companies. He's been moving money around to cover others while selling off some of their joint possessions."

"For instance?" she asked, more than a little surprised by the news.

"They kept a small yacht up at Lake Texoma," he stated. "It's been sold for a price well under market value, which is a big red flag to someone's financial position."

"They loved that yacht," she said. "Tried to get me on it several times but I couldn't imagine being stuck on a small boat with my sponsors for hours on end."

"Erik's interest in you most likely aided that decision," he added.

"There's a lot of truth there," she agreed. "It wasn't hard to turn down."

"I can imagine," he stated. "Besides having money troubles, their marriage is on the rocks. But Erik might not know it yet."

"How so?" she asked.

"Ashley has been secretly meeting with an aggressive divorce attorney," he added.

"How long has that been going on?"

"Since not long before you picked up a stalker," he confided.

"Is it possible the stalker is really someone watching me to see if Erik and I are having an affair?"

She picked up her coffee mug and palmed it, warming her hands.

"I had the same thought," he admitted.

"It would explain why he was always in the shadows," she continued. "It could have been a private investigator or a random person hired to watch through Ashley's attorney. He could have been trying to dig up dirt."

"Except, why escalate?" he asked.

"To scare me into my boyfriend's arms maybe," she answered. "They could have been trying to push my buttons to see where I went. Most would go to the person they were being intimate with."

"Matrix discovered Erik's calendar dates don't match up with the stalker's," he said with a nod and a look of disdain. Last night, he'd seemed to want her close again after another round of freeze. "Erik can be ruled out."

"That's progress, at least," she said, doing her best not to get caught up in her desire for Sean. Her heart argued differently. It wanted to ride the tide of ups and downs. She wasn't falling into that sinkhole if she could help it. "Is there a chance he was hiring someone to watch me? He hasn't made a secret out of his affection, and he sounds like he was on an emotional ledge between finances and balancing it all."

"I kept him on the list," he said. "Matrix has shifted her focus to digging around in Ashley's personal accounts to see what else can be found there."

"Some of the papers I signed weren't digital," she said. "Some had to be done in person. I have copies back at my apartment but it's probably too risky to go there. Surely the heat is up and someone is watching my place."

"Good to know," he said before picking up his phone and firing off a text. He seemed satisfied when he set the phone down.

She probably didn't want to ask what he was doing or who he was reaching out to, figuring this was on a need-to-know basis like in the military. His was a life of secrets.

"Ashley and Erik weren't the greatest actors," he pointed out. "Both were surprised when you showed up. Ashley seemed like she was trying to cover the most."

"She stuck out in our minds, but we believed it

might be about me having an affair with her husband," Raelynn stated.

An icy chill raced down her spine thinking Ashley could be behind the stalking. Several reasons for the move came to mind now that Raelynn knew about the pending divorce. It was possible Ashley wanted revenge as she walked out by ruining one of Erik's last threads of financial hope.

Love could leave destruction in its wake.

Chapter Nineteen

There were two names at the top of the suspect list: Ashley Bradshaw and Drake Johnson. Those were the two evils they knew about. Erik Bradshaw needed to be watched. Sean wanted five minutes alone with the man to make certain he knew just how inappropriate it was to touch a woman who didn't invite him. But that wasn't what they were after right now. It was a sidebar.

"Are you sending someone to go through my apartment?" Raelynn asked as he polished off the last of his coffee and then set the mug down.

"Yes," he said, figuring he might as well be honest. She had a right to know. "Is there anything we should know about the place?"

"Other than the fact my plants are probably dead by now, no," she said. "I haven't been back in weeks and I didn't want to ask my neighbor who usually helps me out in case it would put them in danger. Couldn't risk them being confused for me if the stalker was angry and decided to take this up a notch or two."

"Makes sense," he said, appreciating how she was always looking out for others. Despite growing up under hard conditions, she'd managed to remain kind without resenting the world. She didn't seem to take anything for granted, not her career or the fact she could have ended up bitter over the past.

"Have you figured out how Anton Miles was connected to what's going on?" she asked.

"Mitch might have," Sean stated. Getting information about the tech worker could take time. The coroner wouldn't have the autopsy completed this early, not in a place like Austin where there was a fair amount of crime. Bodies could stack up at the morgue waiting to be processed. It wouldn't surprise him in the least. It would take time for Austin PD to process the crime scene. They would have to send any evidence off to a lab for evaluation. At least they had a positive ID and a place to start. He wondered if Mitch was able to get ahold of a copy of the report.

"Waiting is frustrating," she said. "It feels like I'm not doing anything and that I should at the very least be on the move."

"You're right about not sticking around in one place for too long," he agreed. "Being still while waiting for intel to come in is a lot like watching paint dry. But if you put your hand on the wall too early, you risk ruining the job you've done so far."

"I know," she said, then flashed her eyes at him. "What I mean to say is that I don't *know*, but it's logical. Up until recently, I had zero experience with being on the run and keeping a low profile, whereas you do this for a living."

He nodded. The idea of a peaceful ranch, working alongside his family members, was starting to sound better by the minute. This life of dodging bullets and staying high on adrenaline for days on end was taking a toll. At thirty-four, he was getting restless in his old life. Now that he'd healed most of the scars from the past, he was ready to move on.

The irritating voice in the back of his mind pointed out that if he was truly healed, he wouldn't have tried to keep Raelynn at a distance when he'd been afraid that he couldn't protect her. The revelation was a gut punch.

"While we're stuck here waiting," she said, breaking through his reverie, "tell me more about your family."

He glanced at her cup. It was half full.

"If you're planning to get me talking about my siblings, I'm going to need a refill," he said, letting himself smile despite everything.

"I can wait for you," she said, returning the smile. Those words resonated with him more than he wanted them to. They had him wishing he could rewind and start over with her—this time without the need to keep distance between them.

"I'm counting on it," he shot back, trying to lighten the mood as he took the couple of steps into the kitchen.

The hairs on the back of his neck pricked. Instinct told him to watch his back. He turned and held his right index finger to his lips to let Raelynn know to be quiet. Her gaze widened as she immediately picked up on the cue. She also reached for the knife she'd been holding earlier when he first got home. *Home?* His word choice struck him as odd.

Either way, Raelynn's instincts to protect herself were spot-on. The fact she wasn't the type to sit around and wait to be rescued was sexy as hell. There were other areas of life he'd like to see her take charge in. But foreplay wasn't the kind of thought he needed to be having under the circumstances.

Instead, he reached for his ankle holster to retrieve his Sig Sauer and crouched down low, listening. An almost imperceptible noise came from the garage downstairs. It could be a critter who'd managed to get inside, looking for food or shelter. A barely audible noise would hit Sean's radar, causing the sensation he'd experienced. His time being deployed had given him a sixth sense when something was about to go down. The system wasn't perfect, but he was getting better at not overreacting. Controlling his heightened emotions had been the first step toward recovering when he'd medically boarded out of the military. Turned out, tremors in both hands made him medically unfit to continue his tour of duty.

Sean methodically moved toward the garage door. He cut off the kitchen light before opening the door. He'd memorized the number of stairs and knew approximately how long it would take to get down there. Being vulnerable on the stairs wasn't his best move.

He listened. Something was down there.

Rather than take the obvious route—a route that would most likely get him shot or stabbed—he closed the door without making a sound and crossed the room to the Juliet balcony. He opened one of the doors and climbed down from the balcony. The second his feet hit concrete, he bolted around the building to the garage.

Lights were out in all the neighboring town houses. The streetlamp was on, casting a dim glow around the internal road. Leaving Raelynn by herself caused his gut to clench, but being obvious by taking the stairs could have gotten him killed. Where would that leave her?

Back against the building, he rounded the corner before crouching behind a brown trash bin. There was enough landscaping to move through to keep him hidden if he stayed low. Hell, he'd belly crawl if he had to.

There were no vehicles out of place in the area, nothing parked nearby that wasn't in a slot. This might be an animal scare. His confidence grew as he checked the area and saw a small window that had been broken in the corner. The hole wasn't big enough for a human to crawl through, but a cat could slip through. It was chilly outside. Some critter was most likely seeking heat.

At this point, he could circle back around and crawl up the side of a building, risking being seen. Or he could punch in the garage code and enter through the back. Since there was no sign of anything out of the ordinary, he decided on the code.

As the garage door opened, a light came on, startling a black cat that darted outside. Poor guy disappeared before Sean could stop it.

Back inside, he pushed the button to close the garage and then stood there until it was secure again. The light would automatically shut off by the time he reached the top of the stairs. He double-checked around the SUV, then inside.

At least his pulse was slowing to a reasonable pace after breaking through the ceiling. A few deep breaths helped.

"It's me," he said before opening the door to the kitchen.

"Everything good?" Raelynn asked as he stepped inside. Back against the opposite wall, knife in hand, she seemed ready for whatever might have walked through the door. She'd moved closer to the Juliet balcony than the door to the garage. Smart.

"It was just a cat," he reassured.

"Thank heaven," she said with an exhale that looked like all her tension released with the slow breath. She set the knife on the billiard table and braced herself using her hands.

He closed the door and, without getting inside his head about his next actions, walked over to her and hauled her against his chest. Her hair smelled like citrus mixed with a spring rain, and all he wanted to do right then was breathe her in.

RAELYNN WRAPPED HER arms around Sean's lean body and then turned her head to rest her cheek against a solid walled chest. His unique, spicy, masculine scent overwhelmed her to the point of distraction.

With his arms around her, he held her like he might never see her again if he let go. A little piece of her heart splintered. He'd lost so much. She'd lost so much. Did the broken soul in her recognize the broken soul in him?

She couldn't be certain how long they stood there. They were so close, so intimate that her body trembled against his. At some point, his cell phone buzzed, breaking into the moment. She told herself the interruption was for the best, even though her heart argued against it. Taking a minute to clear her mind after another scare was probably a good idea. Plus, they'd received a lot of new information and she probably should take time to process everything.

Her brain kept circling back to Anton Miles and the tragic loss of life. What would a tech worker have to do with her? Why would he be in Hamilton Pool Preserve stalking her?

A man with a wife, a kid on the way and a professional job didn't seem like the type to fixate on a singer. Then again, the cops would have visited his home by now and might have some clues as to his intentions.

Speaking of her music, her notebook and guitar were back at headquarters. She pulled out her cell phone and listened to the recording she'd made of the song in progress. Focusing on music calmed her nerves. She would be able to think more clearly if she gave herself ten to fifteen minutes to settle while he checked his message.

Moving to the couch, she turned on a table lamp, keeping the lighting low in the room. She turned the volume of her phone down low, too, and pulled up the music clip. She put the cell to her ear and got the refrain inside her head. As much as she preferred notebook and pen, she could use the Notes app to capture lyrics.

Tapping her fingers on her thighs to the beat, she replayed the clip a few times. She got the feeling she always did when she became obsessed with a song. Those usually had the most potential. Audiences always seemed to respond to the ones that seemed to possess her until they were written. This one was close.

A few more lyrics came to mind. She rocked back and forth to the melody and then frantically captured the words that started spilling out. The music and the words needed to be pulled together, but it was all there.

Finishing a song that came from the heart like this one was the most incredible feeling. Being in the zone while performing catapulted her to new heights, too. The only thing that came close to those highs was the few kisses she'd shared with Sean. Those left her lips tingling with desire for hours afterward.

In her life, she was beginning to realize, there'd been far too few kisses that she'd felt all the way down to her toes. There'd been far too little all-consuming passion that threatened to devour her. And there'd been far too few men like Sean. Then again, he'd broken the mold.

He palmed his cell phone and joined her on the couch.

"Anything happen that I should know about?" she asked.

He shook his head.

"Is that the music you were working on back at headquarters?" he asked.

She nodded. "It's not finished yet. I have all the components, but I need to put everything together."

"It's still incredible," he said with a hint of indignation that she was being so modest.

"Now you're just being nice," she rebutted, thinking there was no way he could have heard clearly.

"I'm not nice," he said. This time, there was a gravelly quality to his deep baritone that affected her low in her belly, flooding her with warmth and causing her pulse to pound against the inside of her ribs. No one had a right to be this sexy by saying so few words. It wasn't even the words. He could make the contents of a cereal box sound like pure sin.

"Thank you," she conceded. "I can't wait for you to hear it once it's all put together."

It dawned on her they might not be around each other once this was over, and a sadness took up residence, burrowing deep in her chest.

"I'd like that a lot," he said. There was a reassuring quality to his tone that made her feel better despite the reality they would most likely be going their separate ways soon enough. She could go back to her life and he would pick up where he left off, heading to his family's ranch.

"By the way," she started. "You owe me something."

The desire that darkened his eyes was more temptation than she probably needed right now. It wouldn't take much for her to fall for this guy.

"And what is that exactly?" he asked.

"You were going to talk about your family before we were interrupted," she said.

"The text that came in a few minutes ago was from my brother," he stated. "Ranchers wake up around 4 o'clock out of habit. There's myself, Rory, Tiernan, and Callum on the boys' side. As for the girls, we have Liz and Reese."

"Six kids?" she asked, but it was the shock talking.

"Four boys and two girls," he said with more than a hint of pride in his voice. "I was born in between Tiernan and Liz. Callum is the oldest. Reese is the baby. Rory is the second to youngest."

"You already said you have a mother and a grandmother," she said. "And that your grandfather recently passed away." She lowered her voice when she said, "I'm sorry for that."

He thanked her and then reached out to squeeze her hand like he did when he was offering reassurance. More of that warmth flooded her with contact. Electricity crackled in the air between them, filling the space with the heat of a fireworks finale.

Then he linked their fingers after bringing her hand up to his lips and kissing her knuckles. A roller coaster drop couldn't have caused her stomach to fall so quickly. He settled their linked hands on top of his left thigh.

"Okay," he exhaled. "Here goes. Granny holds nothing back. She has a sharp wit and an even sharper tongue and I never wanted to end up on her bad side, which was impossible for any of us to do because she loved us despite our ways. My mother was and always will be the rock of the family. After my father died when I was in elementary school, she stepped up in a big way. She's a saint as far as I'm concerned."

"You and your grandfather were opposites based on what you said before," she mentioned.

"He was the problem. Duncan Hayes was one of those old men with an almost permanent scowl on his face. In one way or another, he ran every last one of us off the ranch and Cider Creek," he stated. "He was one mean son of a bitch."

"Why did your mother allow him to take over like that?" she asked. "Sounds like she's a strong person."

"My guess is that she was in over her head with six children after her husband died," he said with a shrug. "I haven't sat down and talked with her but I suspect she figured four boys needed some kind of male figure around. She wasn't as close to her father-in-law as my dad was, apparently. But she stayed on at the ranch because it made her feel closer to the man she lost."

"She never remarried then," Raelynn pointed out.

"Nope. Never dated as far as I know, either," he said.

"That's commitment," she said with a little awe in her tone. She didn't know a lot of people her age who came from a good family where the parents loved each other for life, and beyond.

"She and my father were high school sweethearts who started dating at sixteen years old and never stopped," he said. "Even after all us kids were born, I had memories of walking into the kitchen long after dinner to find them dancing cheek to cheek to some old song."

Tears pricked the backs of Raelynn's eyes at the sentiment. It was beyond sweet. It touched her heart. There'd been no evidence of love in the orphanage. Even the odd jobs she'd worked to make ends meet while figuring out her music career were littered with people who came from divorced homes.

"That might be the most romantic thing I've ever heard," she said. "Even after all the years they were together, they still danced."

"After he died in the car crash, she remarked how grateful she was they'd met in high school because it gave them many more years together than if they'd met later in life," he said.

The story touched her heart in a way that had never been stirred before. She could see living a long life with someone like Sean Hayes and being in love until the day they died. The revelation caught her off guard and made her a little bit misty-eyed.

"I didn't even realize a love like that existed outside of the movies," she admitted, tucking her chin to her chest to hide the emotions trying to flood out of her eyes.

"It's rare," he admitted. "I haven't exactly been searching for it all my life, but I haven't readily seen it in others."

"Maybe only a handful of people get to experience that kind of love in a lifetime," she said.

"For some, it might take a lifetime to find anything close," he said. He opened his mouth to say something else but clamped it shut almost as quickly.

Raelynn felt herself falling for the man sitting next to her. She could only hope the landing didn't destroy her.

She cleared her throat, needing to refocus.

"What about your grandmother? It must be hard to lose her husband so recently," she said.

"Granny is on my mom's side and I'm pretty certain she never forgave Duncan for running off her grandchildren," he said with a smirk.

"She sounds like my kind of person," Raelynn said with a smile.

"I think the two of you would get along just fine," he said.

She had a feeling he was right. Too bad the two would never meet. She could use someone like Granny in her life.

And someone like Sean, but that wasn't exactly on the table. Was it?

Chapter Twenty

The sun peeked through the blinds, and Sean realized they'd been up all night talking. He cracked a smile at the thought that this was the rare time he'd spent the entire night with a sexy woman and all they did was talk. When it came to beautiful, kind, intelligent and sexy, Raelynn was in a league of her own. And he'd been content to hold her hand for hours while filling her in on his family.

Well, hell, he guessed there was a first for everything and this was definitely one of those times.

"What's going on in that mind of yours?" she asked with a raised eyebrow, clearly onto him.

There was no way he was coming clean. Instead, he shook his head and smirked as his cell vibrated.

"Saved by the phone," he said, wanting to see Raelynn smile a whole lot more. She deserved to be happy.

He grabbed his cell and checked the screen.

"It's from Matrix," he said. "Anton Miles is Ashley's distant relative. Apparently, Ashley has a burner phone that she's been using to contact him. She's been blackmailing him to help her out because she found out he was having an affair and threatened to tell his newly pregnant wife."

"Is he the one who hired your company, then?" she asked, clearly stressed about this new information.

"I don't have confirmation, but my guess would be yes," he explained. "A stalker would be a good reason to explain your death. And, apparently, she was planning to end his life so this could never come back on her."

"What would she gain by killing both of us?" she asked.

He studied the screen.

"According to Matrix, you signed papers allowing them to insure you for the tour," he said. "They took out a million-dollar life insurance policy on you."

"I don't remember signing a life insur—"

She gasped.

"The documents she had me sign," she continued. "I'm guessing she slipped that one in the pile and I never realized it. She even said something about covering insurance for me this time. I might have glanced at the header of the page and made an assumption."

"She planned to blindside Erik with the divorce, so I'm guessing she'd already figured a way to cut him out of the insurance money," he said.

"All she would have had to do was sign herself up as the sole beneficiary," she stated. "If memory serves, she was the primary contact on all business relating to me."

He nodded as another text came in.

"According to our tech contact, an airline ticket has been purchased in Ashley's name. She is headed to DFW Airport now," he said. "We have to stop her from getting onto the flight."

"Can't we call the police?" she asked, standing up.

"By the time we explain everything, and they alert airport police, she'll be on a plane out of the country," he said. "We have to get dressed and go now."

There was no way he was leaving Raelynn here alone to fend for herself on the off-chance Ashley hired someone to finish the job.

"I'll change and be right down," she said before disappearing upstairs.

Sean needed to throw on a shirt, so he was a few seconds behind her. They met in the hallway and headed to the second level together. He strapped on his ankle holster as she grabbed a knife. If he had a second weapon, he would trust her with it. Unfortunately, that wasn't the case here. She seemed determined not to be caught off guard and he couldn't blame her for it. Ashley had been coming after Raelynn.

The lug nut had to have been bad timing. There was no way Ashley could have pulled it off. As for the person responsible for hitting Mitch's computer with the hint about Raelynn, that could have been someone trying to be a good Samaritan without stating the suspicion outright.

"Does Erik know about any of this?" she asked after grabbing her crossbody bag and then tucking her cell phone inside.

"There is no evidence of his involvement up to this point," he confirmed.

Raelynn immediately jumped in the passenger seat as he rounded the front of the SUV after using the garage door opener.

"Can't say he's a good person, but at least he isn't trying to kill me," she admitted. "I never liked Ashley to be honest. My radar was always up with her. Can't say I expected *this*."

"Bad people in dire situations do desperate things sometimes," he said as he backed out of the garage. He hopped out of the SUV long enough to punch the code in to close it again before reclaiming the driver's seat. From this location, the easiest way to get to the airport would be to hop on to Loop 12 to Highway 114.

Ashley, on the other hand, would most likely take the Interstate 635 route, which would circle around straight to airport property. The flight information was on hand. He knew where she would most likely park, so he needed to get there first. With airport security being so tight, intercepting her in a garage would draw a whole mess of unwanted attention. was there a way to get to her before she rounded the curve?

"Where are we headed?" Raelynn asked.

He told her the plan. She nodded, white-knuckling the knife handle. Her other hand tapped on her thigh. Was he putting her in danger by bringing her?

As he merged onto the interstate, the gas light came on. He bit back a curse at the timing. An idea struck.

"We have to stop for gas and I'll need to reach out to Mitch to see if anyone is nearby," he said to Raelynn. "What do you think about staying at the convenience store while I track her down? You'd be surrounded by people and that would provide a safer environment than I could if you stay with me."

"What about you?" she asked, then seemed to realize she was asking someone with military training whether or not he could handle the assignment.

"It'll be easier for me to focus if I'm not watching out for you the whole time," he explained, hoping like hell she understood. "You're important and I'd be distracted."

It was the honest truth. She also realized they'd been together all the time when not at headquarters and hadn't exchanged numbers.

Raelynn stared out the front windshield for a long moment before saying, "Give me your phone so I can program my number inside."

He fished it out and then handed it over. She immediately went to work entering her contact information.

"I'm going to send myself a text so I'll have your

information on my phone," she said. "At least we can reach each other if needed."

"I'll be in touch as much as possible," he reassured.

"You already know what kind of vehicle she drives, I'm assuming," she stated.

He nodded.

"I'll try to watch out to see if her Range Rover passes," she said.

It was a decent compromise, and he felt a whole helluva lot better with this plan in place.

RAELYNN FIGURED HANGING back and being a lookout would give her something to do besides pace around a small convenience store for an undetermined amount of time. Her imagination might run wild otherwise. She couldn't let herself think about anything happening to Sean. One-on-one he could handle Ashley without a doubt. The woman had tricks up her sleeves, and Raelynn didn't trust Ashley as far as she could throw her. She might have an accomplice with her, or two.

The gas station and convenience store off the interstate just before N. MacArthur was close enough to get a decent view of the highway. Four lanes of traffic zipped by, lighter than usual. It worked for her. On the service road, they passed by a fast-food taco restaurant. There was a strip of green space in between the service road and the interstate with a four-foot-tall electrical box. She could sit tight there and see the vehicles clearly. Ashley's Range Rover was distinct, with a roof so dark it looked almost deep purple. She had customized license plates, as well.

Thankfully, it was chilly outside so Raelynn wouldn't fry in the sun while taking her post.

"I'll be right there," she said, pointing to a spot as Sean circled the pump. She put the knife in the glove box, figuring she wouldn't need it while on the side of the highway.

"It's a good position," he said, his voice a study in calm. His demeanor changed, intensified like a professional athlete about to step into the arena on game day.

After pumping gas, he returned to the driver's seat.

"You'll be okay?" he asked, some of the confidence drained from his tone.

"Yes," she said. This time she was the one offering reassurances.

He reached over and squeezed her hand.

"Let me know when you see her," he said.

"I will," she said before exiting the vehicle. She moved quickly across the street and took her position as he exited the parking lot. She had no idea what his plans were as she settled into her spot.

A few minutes passed before the first possibility dotted the horizon. As the vehicle got closer, Raelynn saw that it wasn't Ashley. So many words popped into her thoughts about that woman, none of them ones she should probably repeat in public.

Watching the cars, trucks and SUVs zip by, Raelynn wasn't sure how much time had passed with no sign of Ashley's vehicle. It occurred to Raelynn the woman could have used a car service to take her to the airport. On second thought, no, maybe not. She probably made the plans in a rush and would use her own vehicle.

The next thing she knew, a cord came in front of her and tried to wrap around her neck. She brought her hands up in time to stop it from making contact with her skin, but the cord tightened, cutting into her fingers.

She was suddenly being hauled backwards as her cell phone went flying, tumbling to the ground. Her hands were trapped but at least she could still breathe.

"You just won't die, will you," Ashley said as Raelynn was thrown into the back of a white Suburban. Ashley was behind the wheel. A male Raelynn didn't recognize crammed in the back seat behind her.

Raelynn figured she was as good as dead if they took her somewhere else. The only reason they weren't doing it immediately was most likely because blood stains would tie her murder to Ashley. The insurance money would be lost forever and Ashley would end up divorced and broke.

Coiling her leg as tightly as she could, Raelynn released with force. Her heel slammed into the guy who'd crammed her inside the vehicle. Her face slammed against the opposite door at the same time her foot connected with his rib cage. He grunted and then slammed a fist into her hip.

From this angle, she couldn't get a look at him.

"Bitch," he ground out. She didn't recognize the voice, either. Or did she? Hold on a minute. She did recognize the voice. Danny something or other. She couldn't recall his last name except that she remembered he was a lawyer for the Bradshaws.

"Can't you knock her out back there?" Ashley whined as he tried to close the door. His body must have still been partially out the door because it wouldn't close.

"Do you want blood everywhere?" Danny asked.

"You'll be disbarred for this," Raelynn stated.

"Shut her up," Ashley commanded.

"She's just trying to get under my skin, babe," he said as he struggled to get control.

"Close the door so we can get out of here," Ashley said. "People are starting to stare."

Those were the only words Raelynn needed to hear. She jerked a hand free from the cable as he struggled to get control of her. Without wasting another second, she reached up and then opened the door as she kicked like her life depended on it.

It did.

Danny gripped her calf, digging his thumb in until she feared he might break skin. He pulled her toward him with a relentless grip.

She couldn't catch her breath enough to scream. Instead, she writhed and wiggled, trying to force herself out the opened door.

"Do I have to do everything myself?" Ashley's irritation came through loud and clear in her voice. She jammed the gearshift into park, and then climbed down from the driver's side. She circled the front of the Suburban as Raelynn was making progress moving closer to freedom.

The next second, Ashley was there, shoving at Raelynn to get her back inside as Danny pulled from the opposite end. Combined, their efforts were too much for Raelynn to defend on her own.

She was suddenly yanked upright and forced to sit in Danny's lap. His arms came around her like a vise, pressing her back into his so tightly there was no wiggle room. She cursed and yelled for help. Inside the vehicle with the doors closed and the windows up, her screams fell on deaf ears.

"Shut your mouth or I'll shut it permanently," came the low, angry voice from behind her.

She had no plans to make this easy on either one of them. Her arms were unmovable no matter how much she tried. There was only one thing she could do. It had to work.

Raelynn ducked her chin to her chest, and then snapped back so hard she heard a crack.

"Bitch," came out low and in a growl but he released her.

Raelynn grabbed the handle, threw her shoulder into the door and then dropped an elbow into Danny's crotch. The move gave her the leverage she needed to break free from his grasp and get out of the SUV.

Ashley jumped out of the driver's seat. A glint of metal shone in the sunlight. Outrunning her might not be possible. Raelynn screamed for help as she spun the rest of the way around to face her, ready to fight.

The woman got off the first jab. Raelynn felt a sharp pain underneath her left armpit as she attempted to jump out of reach.

Where was Sean?

Chapter Twenty-One

Twenty minutes had passed and there was still no warning from Raelynn. Two had gone without a response to his text, checking on her. He swung the wheel wide and then made a U-turn to head back to where he'd dropped her off.

All his warning signals fired as he gunned the engine, pushing the SUV as fast as it would go. This wasn't good. Something wasn't right. She would have responded by now. Anger instead of guilt threatened to burn him from the inside out.

He exited on N. MacArthur and immediately saw an out-of-place white Suburban. A small crowd had gathered in the parking lot of the Shell station. He fought the instinct to roar up to the scene. Instead, he abandoned his SUV at the light and ran toward the stopped vehicle. There was activity toward the back… A struggle?

The back hatch opened and then he heard a sound that stopped him in his tracks. The crack of a bullet split the air. His heart stopped beating in his chest for a long moment as he darted to the front of the Suburban for cover.

He dropped down on all fours and checked underneath the Suburban. There were three people back there. Two looked to be trying to stuff Raelynn in the back.

A guy with a belly that hung over his jeans ran toward the back of the vehicle holding a gun. No, this wasn't a good sign.

"Stop what you're doing," he said, charging toward the trio. Could Sean use the guy with the belly as a distraction?

He moved around the driver's side of the Suburban in stealth mode.

"Hey," the man said. "Stop."

In the next few seconds, chaos broke out. The crowd in the parking lot panicked, screamed and ran in every direction. The crack of another bullet split the air. It was as though all the air was sucked out of his body. Sean stopped. Make a move now and he could literally end up shot. Or worse. Something could happen to Raelynn.

Coppell PD showed up in full force with three marked vehicles roaring up to the scene. An officer jumped out of his seat, pointed his weapon at the man with the gun and commanded, "Set your weapon down on the ground and put your hands in the air. Do it. Now."

Pot Belly complied before taking a step back. The officer came around his door with his weapon trained on Pot Belly.

Danny dove toward the weapon on the ground,

came up with it and shot the officer. Blood splattered from his neck.

The distraction gave Sean enough time to round the back of the vehicle and grab Raelynn out of Ashley's grip. He stepped in between her and Ashley.

"Everyone, listen up," one of the cops said. "I want hands in the air or we'll start shooting." He turned his attention to the male with the gun. This wasn't Erik. He was taller with more of a runner's build. "Sir, drop the weapon."

Instead, the male opened his mouth, put the barrel of the gun inside and then pulled the trigger. He must have hit the spinal cord just right because he immediately fell limp on the ground. Sean snapped into action. Keeping his hands high in the air, he kicked the weapon away from everyone for safe measure.

Cops descended on the scene, securing the area and taking Ashley down.

Raelynn was on her knees, bent forward, clutching her stomach. The second Sean saw blood dripping down her elbow, time slowed to a standstill. This wasn't supposed to happen. He'd been there to protect her and failed.

His world tipped on its axis and his head spun. Bile burned the back of his throat as he pushed through the guilt that had wrapped around him like a locked straitjacket, making it near impossible to break his arms free.

The scene was like something out of an action film. Ashley was facedown on the concrete, hands behind her back, while a female officer placed zip cuffs on her wrists. Another officer sat on the ground, blank faced, while another officer tended to him, putting pressure on the wound on his neck to stem the bleeding. A piece of shrapnel must have nicked him. He was going to be fine, but his brain hadn't caught up to the fact yet.

The sounds of police radios squawking filled the otherwise still air. But all he could focus on was Raelynn and the blood as he picked himself up and bolted toward her. This couldn't be happening. Not again.

Sean caught himself right there as he dropped down in front of her. She was surprisingly calm, almost eerily so.

"Am I okay?" she asked as the color drained from her face. She searched for reassurance in his.

"We're going to stop the bleeding and you'll be all right," he promised. "You're with me now. I got you. But we need to assess the damage."

He took her hands in his and lifted them up, watching as blood rolled down her arm. He ripped off her left sleeve and saw a gash underneath her armpit. It was deep and a couple of inches long.

Sean shrugged out of his T-shirt, balled it up and pressed it against the knife cut as a welcome siren blasted the air. An ambulance roared up a few seconds later.

"She needs help here," he said, calling over the paramedic who jumped out of the passenger seat. The team split as the driver took off toward the officer.

Meanwhile, Ashley was spewing all kinds of venom and threats in the background as she was being pulled up to standing. The female officer walked Ashley over to the department-issue SUV as the EMT went to work on Raelynn.

"This isn't as bad as it looks," the EMT said. His name tag read Andy. Andy was Sean's new favorite name. Relief was a flood to dry plains. He finally exhaled.

His cell was going off, but he needed to be 100 percent certain Raelynn was going to make it through this and be fine. The thought of losing her wasn't something he could fathom—period. Hell, the thought of being away from her at all tightened a knot in his chest to the point he could barely breathe. Did she feel the same?

Instead, he shot off a quick text to Mitch, letting his know they were fine.

Raelynn reached for his hand, so he moved to her side after linking their fingers. The second their hands clasped, he could breathe again. He was in over his head with Raelynn, and he couldn't let her leave without knowing how he felt.

Andy cleaned the wound and patched her up in a matter of a few minutes.

"You should swing by the ER when you leave here to have the wound properly stitched," he said to Raelynn. "The glue should hold until you get there."

She nodded.

"I wouldn't advise driving yourself," Andy continued. "If you need a ride, you're more than welcome to go with us."

"She doesn't," Sean said before thanking Andy

for everything he'd done. "We'll head over as soon as we leave here."

His cell went off again. Someone was urgently trying to get ahold of him, so he fished out his phone and checked the screen. "It's Mitch. He's worried about you."

"Worried like a parent might be?" she asked, leaning into Sean's side.

"I can ask," he said as Andy excused himself.

"I've decided not knowing is far worse," she admitted. "But I don't want the answer right now."

"Let me shoot him a text to say we're good and Ashley is under arrest," he stated, hating to let go of her hand to do it. At least she'd burrowed into his side, sitting so close he could feel her rapid heartbeat.

After updating Mitch, he immediately linked their fingers again.

"How did she know where I was?" she asked after he ended the call.

"Ashley might have seen me drop you off," he concluded. "Or it's possible they saw you on the side of the road and circled back around. You wouldn't have recognized the white Suburban as hers."

Raelynn took in a slow breath and then nodded.

"Are you ready to get out of here?" he asked, thinking that if he didn't tell her what he was feeling soon his heart might burst through his ribs.

"Can we sit for a minute until I catch my breath?" she asked.

"Whatever you need," he said, surprised she wasn't ready to get the hell out of there.

They sat in silence for a few minutes before either spoke.

"After the ER, I'd like to pick up my guitar and notepad from headquarters before you drop me off at home," she said.

Was that the reason she didn't want to leave? She thought he was going to make sure her wound was properly tended to and then walk out of her life?

The knot tightened in his chest. It was a huge risk to tell her how he felt. But then, he'd regret it for the rest of his life if he didn't. He'd experienced enough regret to last a lifetime. He took a deep breath for courage and decided to go for it.

"What if I didn't take you home?" he asked, catching her gaze and holding on to it. "What if I wasn't ready to be without you?"

"What are you saying, Sean?" she asked. In a few short days, he'd learned to read her based on her facial expressions. This time, she gave no indication of how she felt or if this subject was welcomed. Had he misread the situation? Did it matter if he had? She needed to know where he stood.

"That I can't think of going to sleep tonight without you right by my side, in my arms and in my bed," he stated. "Caution is normally my middle name when it comes to diving in headfirst to a relationship, so I'm just as caught off guard as you probably are that I've fallen this hard for you."

She looked like she was about to speak but then compressed her lips.

"You can tell me to go to hell if you want," he

continued, figuring he might as well go all in at this point. "But I'm in love with you, Raelynn. I want to be by your side, protecting you for as long as you'll allow it."

A tear leaked from her eye, running down her cheek. He thumbed it away.

"I want to be there when you wake up every morning and by your side through all the ups and downs," he said. "But if you don't want the same thing, I'll walk away and let you be."

"I can't imagine a worse fate than losing you," she said to him. The knot in his chest loosened enough to flood him with warmth. "It's not in my nature to stick around in one place for too long and I've never wanted to be with someone for the long haul. I just never saw it in my future."

He nodded, figuring she was about to let him down easy.

"Until you," she said. "I love you, Sean. I don't want to go another day not knowing you or having you right by my side. I'm certainly not perfect and I can't promise life with me will be easy. But I can't imagine waking up another day without you. You're the best thing that's ever happened to me. My soul recognized yours almost the second our eyes met. This is what I was writing about in the song. You. I'm in so deep with you that I should probably be scared. But I'm not. I trust you and I'm head over heels in love for the first time in my life."

"I don't need perfect," he said, bringing her hand up to his lips where he feathered kisses on her wrist.

"I just need all of you exactly the way you are. Besides, perfection is boring. Flaws are what make a person special. Your flaws are perfection to me."

"Then kiss me," she said. "And plan to keep those kisses coming for the rest of our lives."

"I'm all in," he said before leaning over and pressing his mouth to hers. One word came to mind the second their lips touched—*home*, which was exactly where he planned to take her next. "Think you'd like to build a studio on a ranch where you could write songs and record any time you wanted?"

"Is that a serious question?" she asked, practically beaming. "I'd like nothing more than to write songs and, eventually, make babies with you."

He kissed her again.

"Nothing would make me happier," he said, thinking his luck was finally turning around.

Epilogue

Raelynn walked hand in hand inside headquarters with Sean after visiting his home in Cider Creek—a place she would soon call home as well. The facial recognition software would allow her access at any time, but she couldn't imagine being here without Mitch. Her guitar was upstairs along with her notepad. Mitch knew she was on her way, but he was out and would be back soon.

Ashley started spilling all the details after her arrest. Erik had had no involvement in the insurance scam. Her and the lawyer planned to relocate once the policy paid out, giving him plenty of time to set up a practice in Florida. The two of them hired the second guy in the Suburban. He'd been involved in the murder of Anton. His job had been to help cover tracks.

The answer she was searching for sat on top of the granite island, along with a vase filled with lilies, her favorite.

Sean tightened his grip around her hand. The reassurance flooded her with confidence that she could handle whatever the test results read. She'd found her family in him and a lifelong friend in Mitch if he didn't turn out to be her biological father. The man had a habit of taking in strays and holding on to them until they were whole again.

Friend or father? As she approached the island, nerves kicked up a couple of notches. There were two slips of papers, stacked on top of each other. The first one was from the lab.

She picked it up and read the top line. There were three columns, and lots of circled numbers in the columns underneath the headings: Child and Alleged Father.

The box underneath the columns summed it up. *The alleged father is not excluded as the biological father of the tested child. Based on the testing results obtained from analyses of the DNA loci listed, the probability of paternity is 99.9998%.*

She glanced over at Sean, who was smiling. He feathered a kiss on her lips that made her bones melt.

"Congratulations," he said against her mouth.

She kissed him back in response.

The second piece of paper was a letter from Mitch. It read:

Dear Raelynn,

I hope you're as happy about the results as I am. The fact you're my daughter makes my life complete in ways I never understood before I met you. And yet, I've failed you. I'm sorry for letting you down all these years. I'm sorry that I wasn't there for you and you had to endure so much hurt when you deserved to be loved unconditionally and protected by your parents. And I'm sorry that you'll never know the amazing person your mother was. I'd like to fill in your questions about her, if you'll allow me to. Talking about her again makes me realize how much I've missed her all these years. I guess first loves have a way of leaving a permanent mark on the heart.

I have a lot of lost time to make up for with you. It's my sincerest hope that you'll let me.

Love,
Your Dad

Tears streaked Raelynn's cheeks as she finished the letter. She couldn't imagine getting a better draw than Mitch for a parent. And, yes, she was ready to make up for lost time.

She turned and hugged the other amazing man standing right next to her. All the struggles she'd endured in her life didn't seem so awful when she realized they'd led her to this exact moment. As far as she could tell, she was the luckiest woman in the world.

* * * * *

Look for more books in USA TODAY *bestselling author Barb Han's The Cowboys of Cider Creek miniseries coming soon!*

And if you missed the previous titles in the series, Rescued by the Rancher *and* Riding Shotgun *are available now wherever Harlequin Intrigue books are sold!*

COMING NEXT MONTH FROM

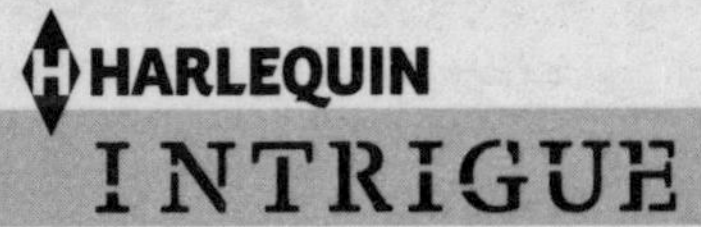

#2151 TARGETED IN SILVER CREEK

Silver Creek Lawmen: Second Generation • by Delores Fossen

A horrific shooting left pregnant artist Hanna Kendrick with no memory of Deputy Jesse Ryland...nor the night their newborn son was conceived. But when the gunman escapes prison and places Hannah back in his crosshairs, only Jesse can keep his child and the woman he loves safe.

#2152 DISAPPEARANCE IN DREAD HOLLOW

Lookout Mountain Mysteries • by Debra Webb

A crime spree has rocked Sheriff Tara Norwood's quiet town. Her only lead is a missing couple's young son...and the teacher he trusts. Deke Shepherd vows to aid his ex's investigation and protect the boy. But when life-threatening danger and unresolved romance collide, will the stakes be too high?

#2153 CONARD COUNTY: CODE ADAM

Conard County: The Next Generation • by Rachel Lee

Big city detective Valerie Brighton will risk everything to locate her kidnapped niece. Even partner with lawman Guy Redwing, despite reservations about his small-town detective skills. But with bullets flying and time running out, Guy proves he's the only man capable of saving a child's life...and Valerie's jaded heart.

#2154 THE EVIDENCE NEXT DOOR

Kansas City Crime Lab • by Julie Miller

Wounded warrior Grayson Malone has become the KCPD's most brilliant criminologist. When his neighbor Allie Tate is targeted by a stalker, he doesn't hesitate to help. But soon the threats take a terrorizing, psychological toll. And Grayson must provide answers *and* protection to keep her alive.

#2155 OZARKS WITNESS PROTECTION

Arkansas Special Agents • by Maggie Wells

Targeted by her husband's killer, pregnant widow and heiress Kayla Powers needs a protection plan—pronto. But 24/7 bodyguard duty challenges Special Agent Ryan Hastings's security skills...and professional boundaries. Then Kayla volunteers herself as bait to bring the elusive assassin to justice...

#2156 HUNTING A HOMETOWN KILLER

Shield of Honor • by *Shelly Bell*

FBI Special Agent Rhys Keller has tracked a serial killer to his small mountain hometown—and Julia Harcourt's front door. Safeguarding his world-renowned ex in close quarters resurrects long buried emotions. But will their unexpected reunion end in the murderer's demise...or theirs?

YOU CAN FIND MORE INFORMATION ON UPCOMING HARLEQUIN TITLES, FREE EXCERPTS AND MORE AT HARLEQUIN.COM.

HICNM0523